A THIEF IS ON THE LOOSE!

There was a hum of anticipation as Max began to explain the rules of the Mystery Weekend to the Pony Clubbers.

"Clues have to be left where they're found so that other riders can find them. But a team doesn't have to tell about a clue. It's perfectly okay to keep that information secret. On Sunday, at our final lunch, the prize will be awarded. And now . . ."

There was a clatter on the stairs. The riders turned.

May Grover appeared. Her eyes were red. Her cheeks were tear-stained.

"The worst . . . ," she said, and started to cry.

"What?" said Max.

"My saddle is gone!" May wailed.

THE SADDLE CLUB

MYSTERY RIDE

BONNIE BRYANT

A BANTAM SKYLARK BOOK
NEW YORK · TORONTO · LONDON · SYDNEY · AUCKLAND

RL 5, 009–012

MYSTERY RIDE

A Skylark Book / October 1995

Skylark Books is a registered trademark of Bantam Books,
a division of Bantam Doubleday Dell Publishing Group, Inc.
Registered in U.S. Patent and Trademark Office and elsewhere.

"The Saddle Club" is a registered trademark of Bonnie Bryant Hiller.
The Saddle Club design / logo, which consists of
a riding crop and a riding hat, is a
trademark of Bantam Books.

ISBN 0-553-48266-1

Published simultaneously in the United States and Canada

Bantam Books are published by Bantam Books, a division of Bantam Doubleday
Dell Publishing Group, Inc. Its trademark, consisting of the words "Bantam
Books" and the portrayal of a rooster, is Registered in U.S. Patent and
Trademark Office and in other countries. Marca Registrada. Bantam Books,
1540 Broadway, New York, New York 10036.

PRINTED IN THE UNITED STATES OF AMERICA

OPM   0 9 8 7 6 5 4 3 2 1

I would like to express my special thanks
to Helen Geraghty for her
help in the writing of this book.

1

"I THINK WE saw that maple tree half an hour ago, except it had twice as many leaves," Lisa said. She looked down. The ground under the tree was carpeted with a ring of newly fallen yellow leaves.

"I'm totally sure we did," Stevie said. "Kind of."

The members of The Saddle Club, Lisa Atwood, Stevie Lake, and Carole Hanson, groaned. It was a crisp, cool Thursday afternoon in late fall. The next day was the beginning of the Mystery Weekend at Pine Hollow Stables, where the girls rode. The MW, as they'd taken to calling it, was going to last from Friday afternoon to Sunday morning. Max Regnery, the owner of Pine Hollow and head of their Pony Club, Horse Wise, had said the MW would involve a pretend mystery and lots of riding.

Carole, Lisa, and Stevie had ridden out to inspect the trails so that on Friday they would notice any freshly planted "clues." But now the girls were busy wondering if they had kicked off the MW by getting lost in the woods. If they had, the other members of Horse Wise would never let them forget it. Especially snooty Veronica diAngelo.

The Saddle Club had never ridden in a Pine Hollow MW before, and the girls were confident they would be the ones to solve Max's mystery. Even though he had told them not to expect too big a prize, they felt their honor was at stake. After all, weren't they the ones who had solved the horsenapping during a three-day event at Pine Hollow? And hadn't Lisa prevented a horse-poisoning before the famous Preakness race? And wasn't Stevie known as the wiliest fox around during their mock fox hunts? Even if it was only a game, the MW was right up The Saddle Club's alley.

"I'm sure I remember those toadstools," Stevie said. "And that skunkweed is almost totally familiar."

"Yes, but which way is the stable?" said Lisa.

They stared into a grove of birch trees. In fall everything changed. Familiar landmarks, such as rocks, were buried under blankets of leaves; wild asters turned white, and blackberry bushes turned into twisted purple stems.

"I bet Carole knows," Lisa said. Carole knew everything there was to know about horses, so—it stood to reason—Carole would know how to get back to the stable.

"Well," Carole said with a weak grin, "we're definitely in the woods behind Pine Hollow, and"—she rubbed her chin judiciously—"I would say that we're definitely on a riding trail. And furthermore, I would say we're definitely on horseback. Right, Starlight?" She reached down and gave her dark bay horse a pat.

"Great," Stevie said. "We promised Max we'd keep an eye on the younger riders, but we can't even keep an eye on ourselves."

Carole looked up. Overhead a hawk was circling, making high-pitched cries. Carole noticed that the sun caught its belly. She knew this meant that the sun was low. She looked at a birch tree and saw that its leaves were transparent with light.

"That must be west," she said, pointing, "because the light is coming from over there."

"Yes!" Stevie said. "So that must be the way back to Pine Hollow."

They turned their horses and rode toward the light of the setting sun.

"Fall's almost over," Carole said sadly. "And spring is about a million years away."

"One last beautiful weekend," Lisa said.

"And then mud," Stevie said.

"And ice," Carole said. In winter Horse Wise mostly rode in the indoor ring at Pine Hollow. That was fun, but it wasn't the same as the glorious freedom of the trail.

"We'll have to make the MW great for everyone, especially the little kids," Carole said. She remembered that when she was a kid, riding at Marine Corps bases, winters seemed practically infinite. Even though many of those Marine Corps bases had been farther south, she'd gotten used to trails that turned muddy and treacherous in winter. "We have to make sure the kids' ponies are properly tacked up. And that they don't gallop." It was a rule of the MW that no one was allowed to gallop. "And we have to help them with their clues so they don't get frustrated."

"And we have to keep them from getting lost in the woods like us," said Stevie with a grin. The Saddle Club would be glad to help the younger riders. That task would fit in with the club's two rules—members had to be totally horse-crazy, and they had to help out when there was trouble.

"A.J.'s coming to the MW," Stevie added. A.J. was a rider from Cross County, a Pony Club in a nearby town.

4

He was famous for his practical jokes. He was also best friends with Phil Marsten, Stevie's boyfriend.

"And?" said Lisa with a grin.

"And he's bringing his friend Bart," Stevie said.

"And?" said Carole.

"No Phil," said Stevie dejectedly. "We had a three-hour phone conversation last night. He was planning on coming, but his grandmother is sick and his family is going to visit her. His mother even came on the phone to tell me how sorry she was."

"That's a bummer," said Lisa sympathetically.

"Totally," Stevie said. "I was counting on outwitting Phil this weekend."

"You can always outwit him another weekend," Carole said.

"It's not the same," said Stevie, looking at the golden woods. She had anticipated riding with Phil down these trails and maybe stealing some time alone with him.

As they came around a curve in the trail, the woods opened onto a large field. On the edge sat a dark barn with a shingled roof and a padlocked door.

"We have to make sure the younger kids stay away from these barns," Carole said. "The park uses them to store machinery, so they're off-limits to everyone but park employees." Silverado State Park included the woods and the mountains behind Pine Hollow Stables.

"We also have to make sure the kids understand that the fields around the park aren't public," Carole said. "They belong to neighboring farms. People let us ride through them as a favor, so it's our job to be careful."

"Wow, look at that," said Lisa, pointing at a tall black shape in a stand of aspen.

"Creepy," Carole said.

"Yes," Stevie said with a grin. "It's a terrifying pump." As they rode closer they saw that it was indeed an old water pump with a curved handle.

"Who would put a pump in the middle of the woods?" Lisa asked.

"Some of these woods used to be farmland," Stevie said. "So they're full of odd things."

Lisa shivered. In the fading light the silvery foxtail grass looked gray. She remembered that this time of year the days were getting shorter, and that when night fell the temperature dropped rapidly. "How far from Pine Hollow are we?" she said.

"Mmmm," Carole said. "I think I smell hickory smoke." The three of them sniffed.

"How do you know it's hickory?" said Lisa.

"It has a kind of tangy smell," Carole said. "And wasn't

somebody explaining to us that hickory smoke is the best smoke?"

"Max!" Lisa said. Just the other day Max had been laying in a supply of hickory logs on his side porch.

"What do you want to bet that Deborah has started a fire?" Carole said. Deborah was Max's new wife, and this was their first winter as a married couple. Chances were that they'd spend a lot of time together in front of the fireplace in the house near the stables.

"What a nice thing to come home to," Carole said.

It seemed to the girls that they were almost back at Pine Hollow. The horses must have felt the same way, because their tails switched contentedly, and they walked a little faster.

"Prancer's thinking oats," Lisa said. "She's thinking a rubdown." Prancer's ears twitched.

"Max says that horses can't understand English, but sometimes I wonder," Carole said.

Suddenly Starlight shuddered and danced sideways. Stevie's horse, Belle, bobbed her head. Something was wrong. The girls were alert, leaning forward in their saddles, scanning the underbrush, wondering what had spooked the horses.

Prancer whinnied. "Easy, easy," Lisa murmured. As an

ex-racehorse, Prancer was more skittish than the others, and more likely to take off.

The girls looked ahead. Trail dust rose through the trees. There was the sound of hoofbeats.

"Hello," Carole called. This time of evening, when the trails were mainly deserted, the other rider should have greeted them. He was showing bad trail manners.

"What was that?" Lisa said.

"Maybe it was a beginner," Stevie said. The woods, after all, were used by many people, and not all riders knew the rules of the trail.

The horses were still nervy, especially Prancer, who took tiny, bouncy steps.

"Maybe it was just the wind," said Lisa, "or a jackrabbit."

Carole shook her head. She was sure those had been hoofbeats.

Stevie grinned and said, "It seems like the Mystery Weekend is starting early."

2

ON FRIDAY STEVIE rushed home from Fenton Hall, her private school. She had been looking forward to the MW, but now she was *really* looking forward to it. Veronica diAngelo, who went to Stevie's school, had remarked that The Saddle Club might have the brawn to win horse shows and cross-country events, but it didn't have the brains to win an MW. That was enough to make up Stevie's mind. The Saddle Club *had* to solve the mystery first.

She dumped her books on the crowded desk in her bedroom. She had explained to her teachers about the Mystery Weekend, so they had given her extra homework during the week. Now she had practically no homework. She couldn't believe she had been so well organized. Only desperation could make her ask for schoolwork ahead of time!

It was going to be a great weekend, Stevie thought as she changed into her riding gear. She grabbed her pajamas from the back of the desk chair, where she had tossed them that morning, and stuffed them into a bag, adding extra clothes for Saturday and Sunday. It would be a perfect weekend, if only Phil were coming. She dialed Phil's number, but no one answered. She was disappointed, since she had been hoping to have one last chat with him before he went to his grandmother's. Instead she left a message telling Phil she hoped his grandmother was better, and she told a couple of knock-knock jokes that he could pass along. Stevie believed in the healing power of knock-knock jokes.

When Stevie got to Pine Hollow, she stopped off to see Belle. The bay mare was chewing hay from her hay net and looking thoughtful. Stevie let herself into the stall for a chat.

"I'm counting on you, Belle," Stevie said as she reached up to tickle the spot under her mane that Belle liked best. "We're going to need your brainpower this weekend."

"Honestly, Stevie," Lisa said, looking into the stall. "Are we going to need the horses' brains?"

"Veronica said The Saddle Club is too dumb to win the MW," Stevie said.

Lisa laughed and said, "If all we have to do is surpass Veronica's brainpower, we're a shoo-in."

Belle snorted as if she were in total agreement.

"Let's go find Carole," Stevie said.

She and Lisa walked to Starlight's stall, and there, sure enough, was Carole. Carole was brushing the star in the center of the gelding's forehead. It was a funny coincidence that all three members of The Saddle Club rode bays.

"Veronica says The Saddle Club is too dumb to win the MW," said Lisa, peering over the stall door.

"Really? Well, Miss Know-It-All is here already," Carole said. "Making a terrible ruckus."

"Already?" said Stevie in surprise. Veronica wasn't one to help with preparations. In fact, one of her favorite tricks was arriving at the last minute, after everyone else had done the work.

"She just showed up—with a carful of beauty aids," Carole said.

"Too bad there's no such thing as beauty aids for the

11

personality," Stevie said. "Although, actually, she's beyond help." Carole and Lisa giggled.

"She wants to set up her stuff in the loft," Carole said, "and she's complaining because it isn't ready."

Carole, Lisa, and Stevie looked at each other. Veronica diAngelo was the most annoying human being who ever lived, and she had no business complaining that the loft wasn't ready. On the other hand, they had promised Max that they would sweep it out.

"Better get ready for Queen Veronica," said Carole with a sigh.

They walked down the aisle of the barn to the side that held the tack room, the equipment room, and the feed room. They took three brooms from the equipment room and climbed the stairs to the loft.

"Wow," Lisa said as she caught sight of the view out the window. "From here you can see everything."

"You can see the mountains," said Carole, looking left toward the jagged outcroppings of the Silverado Mountains.

"And the water," added Lisa, staring toward the curly silver ribbon of Willow Creek.

"And the mysterious forest that is probably already filled with clues," Stevie said.

"This is taking forever," came Veronica's strident voice

from the parking lot below. Stevie looked down and saw Veronica standing next to her mother's white Mercedes, along with a makeup case, a collapsible dressing table, a large suitcase, a pink hair dryer, a curling iron, and a jumbo battery pack.

"Let me guess, it's a yard sale," said Stevie from the window.

Veronica tossed her shiny black hair and glanced up at Stevie. "I'm not planning to look like a disaster all weekend, unlike certain other people," she snapped.

"So you brought your own ugly salon," Stevie said.

Jackie and Amie, two younger riders who had been listening, collapsed in giggles. Stevie was about to let loose with another insult when she saw Max listening with his arms crossed. Max did not like it when The Saddle Club teased Veronica.

Stevie retreated from the window.

Carole and Lisa were tugging bales of hay into the center of the loft to make a divider between the boys' side and the girls' side.

"Where should The Saddle Club sleep?" Carole said.

"Next to the windows," Stevie said, "so we can get plenty of fresh air. Otherwise Veronica's hair spray might kill us."

As they hauled their bedrolls up the stairs, and then

13

their overnight bags, Lisa said, "Where should we put Veronica and her pals?"

"The younger kids should be near us so that we can keep an eye on them," Carole said, "so I guess Veronica and her friends go at the back."

They looked out the window and saw that Veronica was no longer alone. Horse trailers were pulling into the stable yard. The horses from the Cross County Pony Club were being stabled in temporary stalls that Max had set up on the back paddock.

It was easy to spot A.J. with his bright red hair. He was unloading his horse from his family's van. He looked up and grinned.

"Hey, Stevie," he called. "Ready to make like Sherlock Holmes?"

"Time will tell," she said.

At that moment A.J.'s horse, a gray mare called Crystal, let loose with a bloodcurdling whinny.

Unloading horses was the trickiest part of any sleepover weekend at Pine Hollow. It was especially tricky if the horse was used to another stable, like Crystal. Stevie scrambled down the steps into the yard and walked casually over to Crystal to try to calm her.

Crystal's eyes were rolling, and she looked as if she was

about to take off. Stevie decided to try another method of calming.

"Crystal, I've got a knock-knock joke for you," she said.

A.J. shook his head and said, "I don't believe this."

"Knock knock," Stevie said.

Crystal snorted.

"Sam and Janet," Stevie said.

Crystal pawed the ground delicately with one hoof.

Stevie put back her head and sang, "Sam and Janet evening," to the tune of "Some Enchanted Evening."

For a second there was absolute quiet, and then Crystal shook her head as if she were trying to get the sound out of her ears. But the horse was now calm.

"I didn't know humans could sound like that," said A.J. in an awed voice. "That was *singing*, right?"

"You should hear Stevie's father," Lisa said. "He even whistles off-key."

"Hey, it worked," Stevie said. Crystal was looking around for something to munch on.

"Thanks, Stevie," A.J. said. "That really could have been a mess." They both knew that if one horse started to spook, the others would have followed, and soon it would have been a nightmare.

"I like to add happiness to the world whenever I can,"

Stevie said, thinking that A.J. was going to be fun to have around this weekend.

Something caught Stevie's eye. Someone familiar was standing in the entrance to the barn. Stevie turned to get a better look, but the person, who was wearing a red sweater, vanished into a stall.

A.J. caught Stevie's arm. "Are you planning to lead the singing tonight?"

"I don't want to give the little kids nightmares," Stevie said.

"Stevie," came a voice from above her head, "you've got to see this." Stevie looked up. There was Lisa, her head poking out of the loft window.

"What?" Stevie said.

"It's something I can't describe."

Stevie headed for the stairs to the loft.

Veronica diAngelo had set up a cot with an air mattress; a collapsible dressing table, with a mirror and room for her to spread out her hair stuff and makeup; and the battery pack for her hair dryer and curling iron.

"You're going to be a knockout, Veronica," Stevie said. "When people see you, they're going to knock and scream, 'Let me out.'"

"Ha, ha," said Veronica.

"There's only one problem," Lisa said. "Pine Hollow has

only two bathrooms for all of us, and there's no shower. How can you blow-dry your hair if you can't get it wet?"

"I have an idea," Stevie said. "We could provide you with a bucket."

"And you could soak your head in it," said A.J., who had come up the stairs just in time to hear Stevie's line. Ever since Veronica had tried to sabotage the Starlight Ride one Christmas Eve, A.J. had detested her. But at least, Carole thought, A.J. didn't have to deal with Veronica every day.

As the rest of the riders filtered upstairs, the noise and confusion and excitement transferred itself from the yard to the loft. Carole struggled to help the younger boys get their sleeping bags arranged.

"Order!" came Max's commanding voice from the other side of the loft.

Yes, Carole thought, *order is what we need*. She and the younger boys walked to the other side of the loft, where everyone was staring in amazement at Veronica's portable beauty salon.

"It's like a horror movie," said Ian wonderingly. "It's like *Frankenstein*."

"The Bride of Frankenstein!" said his friend Peter Allman.

Everyone laughed, except for Veronica's friends Polly

Giacomin and Betsy Cavanaugh. Just about everyone in Horse Wise had had a run-in with Veronica.

Max looked around the circle with stern blue eyes. "A crime has been committed this very afternoon. In this very stable."

A murmur of excitement ran through the riders.

"It is a crime of great seriousness," Max said. "The criminal must be unmasked and punished."

"Yes!" said Amie.

"I challenge you to form Mystery Teams of two and three," Max said.

The members of The Saddle Club gave each other high fives. Until this moment they hadn't been sure whether they'd be stuck on a team with Veronica or one of her friends. Now they had their own Dream Team.

A.J. and Bart, who were good buddies, became a team of two. Seeing them together gave Stevie a twinge of sadness, because if Phil were there, he would have been with them. Veronica, Polly, and Betsy made another team. Amie, Jackie, and Jessica made another, and so did Peter, Ian, and Robbie. Jasmine and Corey said they would make a team with May Grover, who hadn't come yet. Within seconds the teams were sitting in groups on the floor, waiting for Max to give them instructions.

"To solve this crime you will need good horse sense,

18

good horsemanship, and brilliant detective work," Max said.

Carole noticed that Amie, Jackie, and Jessica were looking nervous. She resolved to help them as much as she could.

"First, the mystery rules," Max said. "Clues have to be left where they're found so that other riders can find them. But a team doesn't have to tell about a clue. It's perfectly okay to keep that information secret. On Sunday, at our final lunch, the prize will be awarded. And now . . ."

There was a clatter on the stairs. The riders turned.

May Grover appeared. Her eyes were red. Her cheeks were tear-stained.

"The worst . . . ," she said, and started to cry.

"What?" said Max.

"My saddle is gone!" May wailed.

GREAT CLUE, LISA thought. The MW was off to a flying start.

"Was it your new saddle?" asked Jasmine.

May nodded.

"The one your grandparents bought you?" asked Amie.

Tears streamed down May's face.

Lisa was astounded at how well May played this role. Lisa had done some acting, so she knew how hard it could be.

Carole shook her head. Maybe this wasn't part of the pretend crime—it seemed so real, she thought.

"May," came a voice from the stairs. Deborah, Max's

wife, came running to the top of the stairs, her red hair flying. "I saw you crying. What's wrong?"

May dived into Deborah's arms. "My new saddle, the one my grandparents gave me, is gone."

May's saddle was German-made and expensive, Lisa knew. Losing it was a dire event.

"I never got around to putting my nameplate on the back," May moaned.

Lots of riders put brass name tags on the back of their saddles so they could identify them in a crowded tack room.

"It was an Olympia," May said. The other riders murmured with sympathy. An Olympia was ideal for cross-country, with a deep seat and narrow back. For many riders it was a dream saddle.

Max knelt down next to May and said gently, "Start from the beginning, May. Tell us what happened."

"When I got Macaroni, my old saddle didn't fit," May said. May had outgrown her old pony, Luna, so her parents had recently bought her a new one, Macaroni. "And then my grandparents bought me the new saddle for my birthday. It's almost grown-up size," May said. She gulped.

"I know you were taking good care of it," Max said. Everyone at Pine Hollow knew that May was a serious rider who took pride in her equipment.

"It was in the tack room in our stable this morning," May said. "I got up early to clean it especially for the Mystery Weekend. I'm sure I put it back on the rack, but this afternoon it was gone."

"Was anyone home during the day?" Max said.

"My mom," May said. "She was home all day. She didn't go into the barn, but there weren't any cars or anything. The saddle just disappeared." May began to cry again.

"Was anything else taken?" Lisa asked. She knew that May's father was a horse trainer, so the family certainly owned other saddles, probably good ones.

May shook her head. "They didn't take my father's Siegfried." A Siegfried was what was known as a lifetime saddle. Even used, its resale value was excellent. "Or my mother's saddle, which is practically new. Or the CD player."

"I suppose you called the police," said Veronica with a superior smile.

May nodded. "Officer Kent came."

"I know him. He's an excellent officer. What did he say?" Max asked.

"He said there wasn't much he could do. He said saddles are really easy to sell. And . . . and . . ."

"What?" said Max softly.

"He doesn't think I'll get my saddle back."

At this everybody started talking and asking questions, except for Veronica, who stood back with a smug smile on her face to show she was above this melodrama. Betsy and Polly, who were the other members of Veronica's team, looked back and forth from May to Veronica, unable to decide whether to be sympathetic. Their faces changed expression depending on where they were looking.

"It's for real," Lisa whispered to Stevie and Carole. "Max would never involve the police in a fake mystery."

Stevie crossed her arms, looking from May to Max and back again. True, Max looked genuinely worried. But after all, as they all knew, Max could be diabolically clever at times.

"Who says May really called the police?" asked Stevie. "What if it's all part of the fake mystery? After all, we're up against Max."

As if Max heard her, he stood up and said to the group, "I want to impress one thing on you all. May's problem is real. It's not part of the pretend mystery. It's not a game."

"See?" Lisa whispered to Stevie and Carole.

"You forget that we're dealing with a supremely devious mind," Stevie whispered back.

Deborah pulled a tissue from her pocket and wiped May's face.

23

"This doesn't mean you have to miss the weekend, May," Deborah said. "I know your old saddle doesn't fit Macaroni, but you can borrow a Pine Hollow saddle. In fact, I have one in mind, a nice hunting saddle with a square cantle." The Saddle Club exchanged grins. It wasn't long ago that Deborah had been a complete stranger to horses. In fact, she had been nervous and tense around them. Now she was talking like a pro.

"Very convincing," came Veronica's sarcastic voice.

Deborah looked up, annoyed. "Who said that?"

"I did," said Veronica. "You rehearsed this whole thing ahead of time. And I must say you did a very nice job. Those tears were almost convincing," she said to May, who flushed. "You almost fooled me. But you didn't. I can now solve the mystery." Veronica threw Stevie a superior look. "The mystery is that there is no mystery. May's saddle wasn't really stolen. It's all a phony."

"You're a phony," May cried.

This did not seem to bother Veronica in the slightest. "I stand by my analysis," she said smugly. "You can outsmart the others"—she threw another look at Stevie—"but you can't outsmart me."

"I hope someone takes your saddle next, and then you'll know what it feels like," May said passionately.

Veronica tossed her head. "I don't think so." She looked

24

calm, but Stevie could see a flicker of worry in Veronica's eyes. What if there *was* a saddle thief? What if the thief was in the Pine Hollow tack room at this minute?

Stevie gasped. The saddle that she'd gotten for Belle was in the tack room. It was almost new, but already it was beginning to conform to the curves of Belle's back, and it was as comfortable to Stevie as a favorite pair of shoes.

Everyone else must have had the same thought, because there was a mad stampede toward the stairs.

"Riders," called Max. But for once nobody listened to him. The stairs were jammed with riders heading for the tack room.

They rushed through the feed room into the tack room, where there were shouts of joy as Pony Clubbers saw that their saddles were still there. Slowly, the sound of panic changed into happy chattering.

"Whew," said Amie with her arms around her saddle. "At least we can ride out now and look for May's saddle."

Veronica was standing casually next to her custom-made saddle. She was smiling as if she'd never been worried at all.

"I told you there's nothing to worry about," said Veronica, her voice cutting through the happy din. "It's pure, unadulterated nonsense." Suddenly she frowned. "Wait a second," she said. "Something's missing."

"Like your brain?" said A.J.

Veronica looked at an empty rack, wrinkling her forehead. "Whose saddle goes there?" The saddles at Pine Hollow belonged to individual horses. There were no common saddles.

Veronica put a red fingernail on the label underneath the saddle rack. "It's Nickel's," she said smugly. "Someone has stolen his tack."

Everyone in the tack room started talking and asking questions at once.

"Veronica's on a roll, or is that an English muffin?" Stevie muttered. She wished that she had spotted Nickel's missing saddle herself. Nickel was a Pine Hollow lesson pony. A lot of the riders had learned to ride on the sweet-natured dappled gray pony, and he was a big favorite.

"His pad is missing, too," Amie said.

"And so is his bridle," Jackie said.

"That's what I said," Veronica said smugly. "His entire tack is gone."

Everyone turned to May.

27

"Was Macaroni's bridle missing?" Carole asked.

"No," May said. "And it was a brand-new English bridle with laced reins. But his fleece saddle pad was missing."

Lisa noticed that Max was looking calmer. Truly, Max was hard to figure, Lisa thought. The theft of the first saddle had upset him, while the theft of the second saddle seemed to make him feel better.

"This whole thing is crazy," Stevie muttered. "Why would a thief steal Nickel's bridle, which isn't worth much of anything, and leave Macaroni's valuable bridle?"

The discovery of the missing tack touched off another wave of madness as riders checked to make sure that their bridles, martingales, and breastplates were still there.

"This is beyond crazy," Stevie said to Lisa and Carole as they watched the riders mill around. "A thief comes into the tack room and steals Nickel's saddle, which is old and crummy, and his bridle, which is even older and crummier, and leaves a lot of good things behind."

"It's totally strange," agreed Lisa.

"If this thief had any brains at all, he—or she—would have stolen a really good saddle, like mine," Stevie said, putting her hand lovingly on the cantle, the back end of the saddle. It was a full-contact saddle, cut narrow in the middle to let the rider feel the horse. The saddle flaps were curved forward to protect the rider's knees during jumps.

28

All in all, it was a perfect saddle for Stevie, suitable for jumping with its high back and extended flaps, and perfect for dressage with its narrow middle. "Now *that* is a saddle," Stevie said.

"It sounds to me like you want your saddle stolen," Lisa said.

"No way," Stevie said, "but when I go up against a thief, I like to go up against one with a big brain."

"The Albert Einstein of thieves?" Carole said.

"That's it."

Carole could see that Stevie had fully entered into the spirit of things. She was playing this MW for all it was worth.

"Hmmm," said Lisa, pressing her fingers to her forehead. "I feel a thought coming on."

"Yes!" Stevie said. "We could definitely use a thought."

Lisa closed her eyes. "I'm getting a question. Yes. It's coming to me. My question is . . ."

Stevie and Carole leaned close to listen.

"What if someone forgot to put away Nickel's tack and it's still in his stall?"

"Honestly," said Stevie, her shoulders slumping. "That's the least mysterious idea I ever heard."

"But it could be right," Carole said with a grin. "People have been known to forget to put tack away."

"Yes," Lisa said. "When I was a beginning rider, I did it once myself." Lisa didn't like to think back to those early days, when it seemed as if everything she did was wrong.

"So let's check," said Stevie. "But let's do it like proper detectives. Let's do it with stealth."

"Total stealth," Carole agreed.

Casually Stevie put her hands in her pockets and strolled toward the locker room. As she disappeared from view Lisa and Carole could hear her whistling. A moment later Lisa left the tack room and headed into the yard. Carole lingered a moment and then wandered into the feed room. Then, after looking both ways, she walked back out.

Nickel's stall was on the left side of the U that formed the stable. Carole, Stevie, and Lisa, each coming from a different direction, arrived at the same time.

Nickel's saddle wasn't on the rack outside the door. His bridle wasn't on the peg. But that didn't mean anything, Carole knew. Every so often a truly inexperienced rider— or a sloppy one—left a horse's tack inside the stall, or even worse, on the horse.

"Could it be we have a junior Veronica diAngelo among us?" Carole said. Veronica was known for not putting away her gear. In fact, Red O'Malley, the stable hand, usually had to do it for her.

30

Carole opened the stall door. Nickel's stall was empty.

Lisa screamed. Carole blinked. Stevie muttered, "I don't believe it."

In response to Lisa's scream, every rider at Pine Hollow came running. When they got to the empty stall they stared wide-eyed.

"Nickel is gone," Carole said.

"It's getting worse and worse," Amie said. "First they stole tack, now they're stealing ponies."

The riders gasped as they wondered whether their own mounts had been stolen.

This touched off yet another stampede as the riders ran to the other stalls to see if the horses were still there.

"I checked Starlight on the way," Carole said. "He's fine." Lisa and Stevie nodded because they'd checked Belle and Prancer as well.

They stood in the empty stall, listening to the other riders run back and forth. "This is totally dumb," Stevie said. "Who would steal a sweet old lesson pony when there are plenty of valuable horses to steal?"

"You mean you *want* the thief to steal Belle?" said Lisa with a shake of her head. "First you wanted your saddle stolen, and now your horse?"

"No way!" Stevie said. "Belle was stolen once. Do you think I'd want her to go through that again?"

When Stevie first got Belle, it turned out that the mare actually belonged to someone else. There had been a court case with an injunction and a lot of bad feeling. In the end, everything had turned out fine, and the Lakes bought Belle for Stevie. But the whole experience had been upsetting for horse and rider.

By this time relieved Pony Clubbers were coming back. "Nickel's the only one who's missing," Amie said.

"I know Nickel was here a few minutes ago because I stopped to give him an apple," Jackie said.

"So now it's time to look for clues," said Veronica, pushing her way to the front. "Let me see." Thoughtfully she tapped her chin. "It seems to me that Nickel's bucket is gone, too," she said. "And his lead rope and halter."

Stevie felt her face burn. Why did Veronica have to see things first? She wouldn't have minded if any other rider had noticed that the lead rope, halter, and bucket were missing.

Desperately Stevie looked around, hoping to find another clue. A moment later she spotted one.

"Veronica," Stevie said triumphantly, "I think you've overlooked the most important clue of all."

"I don't think so," said Veronica.

"Then what about this?" said Stevie. She picked a piece of red yarn from a splinter on the door of Nickel's stall. "I deduce that the thief was wearing red," Stevie said. "Hmmm." She examined the yarn more closely. "I deduce that it was a sweater." With a grin, she said to Veronica, "Find a red sweater, and you will find the thief."

There was a gasp from the younger riders as they crowded around Stevie to see the yarn.

"Good work," came Max's voice from outside the stall. Everyone turned, and Lisa noticed that Max didn't look as worried as he had before. In fact, he looked downright cheerful. "Everybody come out into the yard, and let's talk," he said.

Out in the cool air of the yard, Max waited until the riders were standing around him in a circle.

"Would anyone like to send out a posse to catch this dastardly pony rustler?" asked Max, grinning widely. Every hand in the circle went up.

"Better get started," Max said. "A pony rustler can travel a long way before sunset."

The riders turned to each other, chattering.

"Before you leave, let's go over the riding rules," Max said. The riders sighed, but they listened because they knew that the rules were devised for their safety.

"Riders must stay in groups of two or three," Max said. "There will be no, I repeat no, riding alone." He looked from face to face to make sure that his words had pene-

trated. The riders nodded because they knew how dangerous it could be to ride alone. "You must observe all the
rules of trail etiquette," Max said. "And you may ride only
on land where we have permission to ride."

"That means stay away from the Biddles'," piped Jackie.

"That's right," Max said. "The fields are privately
owned. We ride there on sufferance. If anyone doesn't
want us to ride in their fields, we can't. And the Biddles
don't."

The riders nodded again.

"Next rule. Riders may not gallop on trails for any reason," Max said.

Stevie stifled a groan. Galloping was one of her favorite
things, but she knew that Max was right. With so many
young riders in the group, galloping simply wasn't safe.

"All riders must return to the stable as soon as Deborah
rings the Pine Hollow bell," Max said. "Night falls quickly
this time of year, so no matter what you've found, even if
you think you're on the verge of a major breakthrough, you
must turn for home as soon as you hear the bell. After all,
you'll have all day tomorrow and Sunday morning to solve
the mystery."

"We can do it," Amie said to her friends Jackie and
Jessica.

"You'll be riding with me," Max said.

"We don't need help," Amie said stoutly. "We can solve it on our own."

"Don't worry," Max said. "I'm not going to help you solve the mystery. I'll follow where you lead. I won't give advice. I'll be there for safety." Amie, Jackie, and Jessica looked relieved.

"Red will go with May, Jasmine, and Corey," said Max.

Stevie turned to Lisa and Carole. "Now the real hunt begins," she said. "Without Veronica there to get in the way, we can really do our stuff."

"At last we can detect," Lisa said as they hurried toward the stable to get their horses. They had only a couple of hours before sunset, and there was a lot to do.

THE THREE GIRLS met at the good-luck horseshoe at the main entrance to the barn. It was a Pine Hollow tradition to touch the shoe before a ride. Maybe it didn't have magical powers, but it reminded riders to be careful, which was probably the reason that Pine Hollow had never had a serious accident.

"Where to?" said Lisa as the girls rode off at a brisk walk.

"Let's go back to the spot where we heard the mysterious hoofbeats," said Carole.

"What hoofbeats?" Stevie said.

Lisa and Carole looked at her with amazement. "The ones we heard yesterday," Carole said.

36

"As in clop, clop, clop," Lisa said.

"Who says those were hoofbeats?" said Stevie airily. "We never actually saw a horse."

"What else could they have been?" said Lisa.

Stevie shrugged. "A couple of branches banging together in the wind."

"Branches don't go clop," said Carole.

"A jackrabbit bouncing down the road," Stevie offered.

"It would have to have been a two-thousand-pound jackrabbit with metal shoes," Lisa said. "How do you shoe a two-thousand-pound jackrabbit?"

"*Very* carefully," Carole said. Lisa groaned.

"Maybe it was a tractor, or a shutter banging in the wind. Or a deer," Stevie said impatiently.

"Maybe it was a creature from another planet, but it sounded like a horse to me!" Carole said. She looked over her shoulder at Stevie. Stevie's cheeks were flushed, and her eyes were bright. Carole knew that look. Stevie had an idea, and when Stevie had an idea, she wouldn't soon give it up.

"Maybe," Stevie said. "But I think that if we want to discover the clues to this mystery, we should ride toward May's house," Stevie said.

"Why?" Lisa said. "Max said that May's saddle had nothing to do with the MW."

"And you believe him?" said Stevie.

"Of course I do," Lisa said. "When Max says something, he means it."

"Not on a Mystery Weekend," Stevie said. "Don't forget that Max is fiendishly sneaky."

"He's not the only one who's fiendishly sneaky," Lisa said with a sigh. "Don't you think there's such a thing as being too clever?"

"No way," Stevie said. She looked at Lisa and Carole with a challenging grin. "Do you want to poke around near Pine Hollow looking for what *might* have been a horse, or do you want some real excitement?"

Carole thought about that. They had spent most of the afternoon in the barn, and she wouldn't mind a nice long ride. The spot where they'd heard the mystery rider had been close to the barn, so searching it wouldn't be much of an adventure. May's house, on the other hand, was on the far edge of the woods.

And besides, Carole could feel Starlight yearning for some real exercise. The sharp fall air had filled him with energy.

"I'm beginning to see what you mean," Carole said.

Lisa, riding last on Prancer, thought that the whole thing was illogical. Max had looked stricken when May announced that her saddle had been stolen, and he had looked happy and relieved when The Saddle Club discovered that Nickel was missing. This could mean only one thing—Nickel's disappearance was the Mystery Weekend puzzle, and the disappearance of May's saddle was real.

"Let's think about the clues in Nickel's stall," Stevie persisted. "His halter, lead rope, and bucket are gone, so that means whoever took him must be keeping him somewhere. And they wouldn't keep him near Pine Hollow."

Lisa realized that Stevie was right.

"And his tack is gone, so whoever took him probably rode him on the getaway," Stevie said. "And because Nickel was still there when the Pony Clubbers went upstairs, he probably hasn't been gone long. So he's up ahead somewhere," she said triumphantly. "He has to be."

"You could be right," Carole said. Suddenly she had a vision of Nickel cantering down this trail.

Stevie turned to Lisa and said, "Are you game?"

"Totally," Lisa said with a grin. But she had another logical thought. "If we canter, we'll miss all the clues."

"We'll trot," Stevie said from the front. "Belle and Starlight and Prancer can trot faster than Nickel can canter, so we're bound to catch up with him."

"Let's go," Carole said.

"Think red yarn," Lisa called out. "Think clues."

Stevie pressed her knees gently against Belle's flanks.

39

Belle nickered and burst into a trot, sending up a spray of dry leaves.

At *last*, Carole thought, urging Starlight into a brisk, exhilarating trot. She knew that if she wanted to be a vet, or a horse breeder, or a trainer, she had a lot of schooling in front of her, but sometimes she wished she could do nothing but ride.

Lisa looked from side to side, hunting for bits of red yarn in the woods. The leaves were gold, orange, copper, bronze, brown, pink, and scarlet—it wouldn't be easy to spot a snippet of red yarn among them.

"Which way?" Stevie called back as she stopped Belle at a fork in the trail. "You're good at maps, Lisa. Which way to May's house?" Carole and Lisa rode up to Stevie.

"I know she lives on the far edge of the woods," said Lisa. "And I know her lawn slopes down to Willow Creek. But the creek curves so much it's not easy to know where it is at any given moment."

Carole and Stevie looked confused.

"What I mean is that I don't have any idea," Lisa said.

"Oh. Me neither," Stevie said. They looked at Carole.

"You're going to think I'm crazy," Carole said, "but I feel like there's a clue here."

"Really?" Lisa said.

"Maybe it's my military background," Carole said. Carole's father was a colonel in the Marine Corps. These days he spent most of his time in an office in Quantico, Virginia, but he'd had training in reconnaissance. "Dad says that if you're really alert, if you really keep your mind on things, you can practically smell a trail."

Stevie started sniffing wildly. "To me it smells mostly like leaves," she said.

"If we can't smell the trail, maybe we can see it," said Carole. She slipped her feet out of the stirrups and waited a second for Starlight to get used to the fact that she would be dismounting. She put her left hand on Starlight's neck and her right hand on the pommel of the saddle. She jumped down lightly, landing on her toes.

"Carole can make even dismounting look great," said Lisa to Stevie.

Carole moved leaves with the well-worn toe of her riding boot. "I see hoofprints," she said. "Lots of hoofprints." She walked to each side of the trail, moving leaves with her toe, bending to look at the soft earth. "Yes," she said, straightening up, "I can say without doubt that horses have been using this riding trail."

Stevie and Lisa exchanged grins. One of the great things about Carole was that, even though she was a terrific rider who knew almost everything there was to know about horses, she didn't take herself too seriously.

"Something tells me we should go right," Carole said as she went back to Starlight's left side and checked his girth.

"The nose knows," said Stevie. "If your nose tells you the trail of the thief goes right, let's follow it."

"No guarantees," said Carole as she swung back up into the saddle.

The trail led through a stand of rhododendrons and past a hollow full of skunk cabbage that was still bright green. Carole thought that one of the best things about these woods was that they had so much variety.

Starlight's gait changed, and Carole saw that there was a puddle in the trail. With true horse wisdom Starlight was minding his steps before he got to the puddle because he knew that the spongy rim could be full of treacherous surprises.

"Mud ahead," Carole called over her shoulder to warn Stevie and Lisa.

Lifting his feet out of the muck, practically dancing, Starlight ventured around the edge of the puddle.

"Hey," said Lisa behind her.

Carole felt a shiver run down Starlight's flanks. "It's just mud," she said to him. "Just gunky black stuff. Ignore it." She knew that the puddle couldn't be too deep, since it was part of the trail. But she wished that Lisa hadn't called out. Starlight had great gaits and high intelligence, but he was also easy to spook.

"I saw something," Lisa said, her voice ringing out in the quiet woods.

That did it. Starlight plunged through the puddle, sending up a shower of mud.

"Uggg!" came Stevie's voice.

On the far side of the puddle Carole leaned over Starlight's neck and said, "Easy, easy."

A shudder went through Starlight. He danced from hoof to hoof, testing the ground. When he didn't sink, he subsided with a grumpy snort.

Carole turned. Lisa had dismounted and was looking at something.

"There's a hoofprint," Lisa said. "I mean, it's not a usual hoofprint."

"You've got to see this," Stevie said. "I think Lisa found your clue."

Carole looked at the puddle. It seemed wide, it seemed inky, it seemed totally treacherous. Then she realized that she was seeing it with Starlight's eyes. Horses may be smart, but they don't know everything. "We're going back," Carole said firmly to Starlight.

Carefully, daintily, he picked his way around the edge of the puddle.

43

Lisa looked up at Carole, feeling rather proud of herself. "This print is fresh," she said. "There's still water in it. It can't have been made more than a few minutes ago."

Carole lined up Starlight with the other horses and dismounted.

"See?" said Lisa.

Carole squatted to look. The hoofprint was sharp. Even more important, it was filled with water. Carole knew that when a horse steps on soggy ground, it's a lot like squeezing a sponge. The hoof's impression fills with water. But then the water soaks back into the earth in a few minutes.

"It's fresh," Carole agreed.

"That's not all," Lisa said. "Take a look at that." She pointed to the back end of the print. Most horseshoes leave prints that are open at the back, but this one wasn't. "That's some kind of weird shoe," Lisa said.

"It's a bar shoe," Carole said, touching the shoe's impression in the mud. "A horse's hoof has to be flexible. It needs to spread when it hits the ground because it's like a shock absorber in a car. Without the flexibility of the hoof a horse's leg bones would break. But some horse's hooves spread and then don't snap back. These horses need a bar shoe to keep the sides of the hoof together."

Carole never forgot a fact that had to do with horses.

"It's a clue," Stevie said. "Trust Max to come up with something brilliant. And trust Lisa to have seen it."

Lisa glowed with pride. Carole and Stevie knew more about horses than she did. But here she had made an important discovery.

"Let's go," Stevie said. "The trail is hot."

"You mean wet," said Carole.

"Definitely wet," Stevie agreed.

Carole and Lisa mounted their horses and headed around the puddle. This time none of the horses objected, because they could sense the riders' excitement.

"Let's gallop," Stevie said. "Sorry, I mean canter," she added, remembering that Max had forbidden them to gallop. "The thief can't be far ahead."

But Carole shook her head. "If we canter, we'll lose the trail. What would have prevented the thief from riding off into the forest and disappearing?"

They looked at the woods. The thief could have gone in a hundred different directions. The girls rode on slowly.

"There's one," Carole said, pointing at a barred print on the edge of the trail.

"There's another," said Lisa, pointing to one on a sandy mound.

They rounded a grove of maples that were almost bare except for a few yellow leaves.

"I see two prints," Stevie said.

The two bar prints were practically filled with water.

"We've got him," Stevie said. "He can't be more than a few minutes ahead." She looked up with a grin of triumph. "I can't wait to see the look on Veronica's face when she finds out we've solved the mystery."

Belle's ears twitched. She sniffed. Suddenly she was acting oddly.

"What now?" Stevie grumbled. Belle was a great horse, but sometimes she could be willful, like when she nipped at Stevie's pockets to see if she had any apples.

"Hey," Carole said. Starlight was dancing sideways.

Then they heard it, the clang of the stable bell. It was faint enough to make them realize how far away from Pine Hollow they had ridden.

"We're almost there," Stevie moaned in frustration. "In five minutes we'll have solved the crime." She looked at the trail ahead with a devilish light in her eyes. "Who would know if we just kept going?" she said. "Wouldn't it be worth it to catch a dastardly saddle thief?"

"Stevie!" Carole said. "Think about horse honor." Max was always impressing on Horse Wise the fact that he couldn't be around to supervise them all the time. For their horses' sake and their own, they had to do what they knew was right. This was called horse honor.

46

"Would Sherlock Holmes have turned back?" Stevie said. "I don't think so."

"Stevie!" Carole said. "We *are* turning back. Do you want to get stuck out here in the dark?"

Stevie looked at the trail ahead. It was tempting. Everyone would be amazed if they solved the mystery on the first night. Veronica would gnash her teeth. On the other hand, the woods at night were dark and cold.

And maybe dangerous.

STEVIE DIDN'T COMPLETELY cheer up until she smelled the pizza.

As Deborah opened the cardboard box Stevie realized that she was starving. The Saddle Club had been out in the woods a long time, and she was ready to eat.

"I don't suppose it has anchovies," Stevie said.

"This one does," said Deborah with a smile. "And it has pepperoni, sausage, onions, mushrooms, olives, and extra cheese."

"Hmmm," Stevie said. "Sounds like an okay pizza." At TD's, the local ice cream parlor, Stevie liked to make wild combinations of ice creams and toppings. With pizza it was the same thing. The more ingredients, the better.

"A Stevie pizza," said Jasmine. "I want some."

"Me too," said May, who was still pale but looked more cheerful.

"Me three," said Corey.

"It's a tribute to your riding, Stevie," said Carole. "They think that if they eat pizza like you, they'll ride like you."

"Then they should eat pizza like you," said Stevie to Carole.

"Too dull," said Carole, looking at the slice of mushroom pizza she was munching on.

Actually, May, Jasmine, and Corey considered themselves the little sisters of The Saddle Club. Anything that Stevie, Lisa, and Carole did, they wanted to do, too.

"You could have normal pizza," said Lisa to Corey, who was bravely chomping on the anchovy, pepperoni, sausage, onion, mushroom, olive, and extra-cheese pizza.

"This is great," said Corey. "I love it."

As soon as Deborah had distributed the pizza slices, the groups gathered in knots around the loft, talking about clues and trying to figure out what to do the next morning.

"Do you hear what I hear?" said Stevie with a grin.

Carole looked up and listened. "It's the sound of whispering."

"Look at Jessica and Jackie and Amie," Lisa said. The three girls had their heads together, talking excitedly.

"They're doing really well," Carole said. "I was worried that they'd have trouble with the clues, but they seem to be digging right in."

Stevie sat back and sighed. "We could have saved them a lot of trouble if only . . ."

"Stevie," Carole said. "The teams don't have to share clues."

"I bet we're the only ones who saw those bar prints," Lisa said. "All we have to do is go back tomorrow and follow them."

"We'll go back nice and early," Carole said.

"But not until after breakfast," said Stevie. "I hear that Max and Deborah are going to cook up something special."

"Like breakfast cereal," said Carole with a grin. She knew that Stevie loved big breakfasts.

"Not cereal," Stevie wailed.

"Well, it might be something better," said Carole.

"Were anybody's horses spooked?" Veronica's voice rose over the whispering.

"A nut hit Macaroni on the head," May said. "He practically jumped out of his skin. I mean coat."

"The creaking of the trees was driving Penny crazy," said Jessica. The onset of the cold fall weather was making the trees groan.

"Garnet didn't have any trouble at all," Veronica said with a smile. "It shows what breeding will do."

"Thank you, Veronica," Stevie muttered. "Just in time to give us all indigestion."

"You mean your horse has breeding?" said A.J., his green eyes wide, his red hair seeming even redder than usual. "That old plug?"

There was a titter around the group because Veronica's horse, Garnet, was a purebred Arabian, and Veronica never let anyone forget it.

"Garnet is the best horse at Pine Hollow," Veronica said. "If you knew anything about horses, you would have seen that right away."

A.J. was an excellent rider. Veronica's comments did not bother him at all.

"Arabs are good for endurance," A.J. said. "And they have good speed. But for true artistry you need a Thoroughbred. They're much better jumpers."

"I've owned a Thoroughbred, thank you," said Veronica.

"And he was a great jumper, right?" said A.J.

At this Carole felt a lump in her throat. She could never forget Veronica's previous horse, a Thoroughbred named Cobalt. Veronica had neglected Cobalt, just the way she did Garnet, so Carole had groomed Cobalt and exercised him and loved him. Cobalt, who was a stallion, was too much of a horse for Veronica. One day Veronica had asked him to take a jump in an impossible way, and Cobalt had too much heart to refuse. His leg had been broken, and he had to be put down.

Unperturbed, Veronica said, "Personally I prefer Arabians. They're so much more aristocratic."

Just then there were footsteps on the stairs. The riders turned and saw Judy Barker, the Pine Hollow vet. She was wearing jeans, as usual, and a down vest. All the Pine Hollow riders liked Judy because she was never too busy to answer questions, and she loved horses as much as they did.

"Judy has something important to tell you," Max said. "It bears on the theft of May's saddle."

With the mention of her saddle, May bit her lip. She looked as if she was going to start crying again.

"I want you to know that you're not the only one," Max said to May. "Judy called to alert us to a rash of saddle thefts, and I asked her to come over and talk about it."

"There have been at least six saddle thefts I know of in the area," said Judy, "and with May's that makes seven, and there have probably been more."

"You mean there's someone who just steals saddles?" said May. "Like it's his job?"

Judy nodded. "It sounds like a professional. Unfortunately, tack theft is pretty common. Saddles last a long time, so there's a big market for secondhand ones."

Carole nodded. "I got mine secondhand." Carole could never have afforded her saddle when it was new. It was beautifully made, with doeskin knee flaps and a square cantle.

"Because there's such a large secondhand trade in saddles, and because they look so much alike, it's hard for the police to trace stolen ones," Judy said.

"I cleaned my saddle before I went to school this morning, and when I came home it was gone," May said.

"That seems typical of this particular thief," Judy said. "Saddles are taken in broad daylight, even when people are at home. The thief takes only one saddle, and it's usually the newest and most expensive one."

May nodded. Because her father trained horses, some of his saddles were worth more than May's, but they had been locked in trunks. Hers was out in the open, along with several of lesser value.

"Sometimes a very expensive bridle is also taken," Judy said, "but nothing else is ever disturbed."

"I have a nameplate on my saddle," Stevie said. "Does that make it less likely to be stolen?"

A couple of other kids nodded.

"That's not enough, unfortunately," Judy said. "Those

nameplates can easily be removed with a screwdriver. The best way to identify a saddle permanently is to engrave your Social Security number in the leather on the underside of one of the knee flaps."

"What if you don't know your Social Security number?" said Amie.

"Ask your mom or dad. They'll tell you," Judy said. "The other important thing is to keep your tack room locked when there's no one in the barn."

"We do that at Pine Hollow," Max said. "I lock the tack room every night—and I'm certainly going to do it tonight."

"I'll tell my parents," May said. "They always lock the tack room at night. I'll get them to lock it during the day, too."

There was a moment of silence while people thought how bad it was to have a saddle thief in the neighborhood.

"I'm sorry to be here on such unhappy business," Judy said. "But I thought you needed to know."

"Thanks," said May, who had conquered her tears. "At least I know I'm not alone. Do you think the police can catch the thief?"

"May, the truth is that these woods are so full of trails it's easy for a thief to get away undetected," Judy said.

"The police are going to need some real luck to catch him."

Jasmine and Corey put their arms around May. They went back to their team meeting.

"What do you think?" said Carole, stretching her long legs.

"It's diabolical," Stevie said happily. "This is the craftiest, sneakiest, most underhanded ploy I've ever experienced. Max should be totally proud of himself."

"You think that Judy's visit was part of the Mystery Weekend?" asked Carole incredulously.

"Of course!" Stevie said.

"You think that Max got May to lie about her saddle being stolen and about calling the police, and then he arranged for Judy to lie, too?" Lisa asked.

"Max has a lot of tricks up his sleeve," Stevie said defensively. "And this is an MW."

"Oh, come on," Carole said.

"Well," Stevie said, raising one eyebrow, "wouldn't it be great if it were true? Suppose Max *has* faked everything? This would be the greatest MW in Pine Hollow's history. In fact, if I were in charge of an MW, this is exactly the kind of thing I'd plan."

Carole and Lisa looked at each other and shook their heads. "Maybe it's a good thing you didn't arrange this weekend, Stevie. Sometimes you have a slight tendency to go overboard," Carole said.

"Me?" said Stevie innocently.

"Let's get back to facts," Lisa cut in. "I'm really bothered by those barred prints. I don't see exactly where they fit in."

"They were fairly large," Carole said. "They'd be too big for one of the smaller ponies, like Dime, but Nickel is sturdy."

"Nickel has big hooves," said Lisa. "I rode him when I was a beginner. I remember when I picked his hooves I was always surprised at how big they were."

"Some ponies have big hooves," Carole said. "Especially ponies that are used in rough terrain. It makes them more surefooted."

"Do you remember what kind of shoes Nickel had?" Stevie asked.

Lisa shook her head. "I've been trying and trying to remember. But I was such a beginner I didn't notice things like that."

"It's a relief your memory isn't perfect," Stevie said. Lisa's great memory was one of the reasons that she got straight A's in school.

Stevie and Lisa looked at Carole. She was a human encyclopedia where horses were concerned.

"I don't know if Nickel wears barred shoes," Carole said. "When I came to Pine Hollow, I already knew how to ride, so I never rode the lesson ponies."

"I've got an idea," Stevie announced.

"Oh, boy," Lisa sighed.

"This is a practical idea," Stevie said. "If none of the other Pine Hollow horses has bar shoes, then the prints must be Nickel's."

"Other horses use those trails," Carole said.

"But these prints were fresh, and we didn't see any other riders. It's late in the fall, so the trails are pretty empty," Stevie said. "Here's my idea. I think you're going to like it. What we do is . . ."

7

MAX APPEARED AT the head of the stairs carrying a saddle and a bridle, a bucket, and a box with two sponges, a chamois cloth, and a tin of glycerine saddle soap. "Time for a tack cleaning demonstration," he said.

There was a chorus of sighs because all the groups had been deep into planning strategies for the next day.

"A saddle lasts forever only if you take care of it," Max said. "Leather cracks unless it's kept pliable."

Everyone knew that was true, so the riders crowded around Max. Even expert riders such as Carole and Stevie knew that there was always more to learn about taking care of tack.

Max placed the saddle on a wooden saddle horse and removed the girth, stirrup leathers, and irons. He turned the saddle over and rubbed the dirt and dried sweat from the leather lining. Then he held the saddle pommel down over the bucket and washed it. When he was done, he dried the lining with a chamois cloth and applied saddle soap. He put the saddle back on the saddle horse, then washed the seat and flaps and dried them.

"Make sure you remove all the jockeys," Max said, pointing to the black greasy marks that had accumulated on the saddle.

Max dried the saddle and then sponged soap into the seat and flaps.

"Don't hold back," Max said. "It never pays to be stingy with the soap."

He dried the saddle to a deep glossy shine, and used polish to clean the metalwork.

The riders murmured with admiration. Not only did the saddle look good, it smelled good. They knew it would feel good next time it was used.

Max held up the bridle he'd brought and said, "Can anyone tell me the part of bridle cleaning that's most often forgotten?"

"Washing the curb chain?" said May.

"That's very good," Max said. "But there's something else that's even more frequently forgotten."

Carole raised her hand, and Max grinned at her.

"Polishing the metalwork?" she said.

"That's good, too," Max said. "But there's something else." Nobody knew, so Max explained. "Polishing the underside of the leather. Just because you can't see it doesn't mean it's not important. Both sides of the leather have to be soft and pliable. Now, who's going to polish this bridle for me?"

May and Corey volunteered, and Max congratulated them on doing a meticulous job.

Afterward came a round of Pin the Tail on the Pony in which A.J. managed to pin the tail to the soft-drink cooler and Veronica managed to pin it on her hair dryer. Then everyone trooped downstairs to check the horses before they went to sleep.

When the riders were back in the loft, Deborah turned off the lights, held a flashlight under her chin, and told a ghost story. Because Deborah was an investigative reporter, she had a gift for making things seem real—and scary. Some of the younger riders got a definite case of the creeps.

Then it was time to sleep. The riders climbed into their sleeping bags, the boys on the left side of the loft, the girls on the right. Deborah was about to turn out the lights when Veronica said, "Not so fast."

"Now what?" said Deborah with a sigh.

"I'm not going to wake up looking like a creep," Veronica said. "Even if other people are." She gave Stevie a significant look.

And then, to everyone's amazement, Veronica sat down at her portable dressing table and proceeded to comb setting gel through her hair.

"I don't believe this," Stevie muttered. "It's going to give the little kids nightmares."

Veronica talked while she combed her hair. "Many people might be discouraged by the fact that there are no shower facilities at Pine Hollow, but to me this is a challenge. If there's no water, I simply use gel." By this time Veronica's hair was shiny with gunk.

"You decided to slime yourself," Stevie said. "If I were you, Veronica, I'd slime myself, too."

The younger riders collapsed in giggles. Deborah, seeing that things were getting out of hand, said, "Make it fast, Veronica."

Undaunted, Veronica continued her lecture. "First you section your hair," she said, poking bobby pins into each hank. "Then you take the first section . . ." She combed a hank of hair straight up.

61

"The porcupine look is very big," Stevie said. "The boy porcupines will be nuts for you." Veronica was a well-known flirt.

Amie laughed so hard she started hiccuping.

"I'm giving you one minute, Veronica," said Deborah. "After that it's lights out."

". . . and then you roll it," Veronica said, twisting the gooey hair onto a roller the size of a hot-dog bun. She finished putting the rest of her hair onto the giant rollers and then turned to look at the other riders.

"I know it looks hard," Veronica said, "but with practice and discipline you can master it, too."

"You look like a Martian," May said.

Stevie, Lisa, and Carole exchanged grins. This was the first time May had been cheerful all day. In her own obnoxious way Veronica had been helpful.

Veronica stood up grandly, as if she were a movie star on Oscar night. "In the morning you'll see what I mean," she said.

"And that's it," Deborah said. "Riders, get in your sleeping bags. Now I want everyone to go to sleep."

That was easier said than done. The younger riders were so excited by Veronica's strange demonstration that they couldn't stop giggling and whispering.

"If you don't get a good night's sleep, you won't be able to find clues in the morning," Deborah said.

That did it. The younger riders subsided. Soon the sound of peaceful breathing filled the loft.

The Saddle Club, however, was wide awake.

"Could you snore a little more softly?" Carole whispered to Stevie.

"The building is shaking," Lisa whispered.

Stevie realized that she might have been overdoing the sound effects, so she stepped her snore down to a low buzz, and then to a hum.

When the breathing of the other riders was totally steady, Lisa, Carole, and Stevie crept out of their sleeping bags and over to the stairs. On the ledge next to the stairs was Deborah's flashlight. Stevie shoved it under her sweatshirt and crept softly down the stairs.

"Unnnnh!" came a muffled sound from behind her. Stevie looked back to see Carole hobbling.

"I never realized hay bales were so hard," Carole hissed. She had tripped over one of the bales in the feed room.

Lisa crept after them, a sweater over her flannel pajamas. They tiptoed past the locked tack room.

The air in the barn was warm and steamy. At the far end of the aisle a horse snorted. Another horse was doing something that sounded a lot like snoring.

Patch was in the first stall. They couldn't just pick up one of his hooves and look at the shoe—it might have frightened him and caused him to lash out. Lisa knew Patch best, because she had occasionally ridden him when she was a beginner, so she walked to his head and said, "I hate to do this to you, Patch."

Through his long eyelashes, the black-and-white pinto stared sleepily at her. Slowly Lisa ran her hand down his leg to his chestnut, the little patch of hairless skin that all horses have on the inside of their legs. She squeezed it gently, and he lifted his foot. Lisa shone the flashlight on Patch's hoof.

"Normal shoe," Lisa whispered.

Patch snorted, and Lisa let go of his foot. Patch gave a long, snorting rumble as he settled back into sleep.

Comanche was in the next stall. Stevie knew him best. She also knew that Comanche had a strong sense of pride and could get riled very easily. "Hoof check," Stevie said sternly as she moved toward his head.

Comanche turned and yawned in her face. He had, Stevie thought, the largest teeth she'd ever seen, and his gums were pretty big, too. Stevie grinned back. She ran a hand down his leg, and without a fuss Comanche lifted his foot.

"Normal shoe," Stevie whispered.

In the next stall Bodoni was asleep on his side. "Hey, pal," Carole whispered. Bodoni snorted and fell deeper into sleep.

"Just like my father," giggled Carole. "The more you try to wake him, the harder he sleeps. In fact, he's an all-around champion sleeper."

"Show time," Stevie whispered to Bodoni. Bodoni blinked. He was a championship horse and loved to compete. "We're having a hoof beauty contest."

Amazingly enough, Bodoni got to his feet. Carole walked in to greet him. She tapped him on the knee, and Bodoni raised his foot.

"Ordinary shoe," Carole said.

"This could take forever," Stevie said with a groan.

As they worked their way down the stalls, Carole thought that it was a lot like being a camp counselor. The horses were either grumpy, sleepy, or irritated. Checking their hooves required a lot of patience.

Finally they finished. None of the horses in the stable had barred shoes.

"So now we know it was Nickel," Stevie said.

Lisa looked unhappy. "Not exactly. What about the guest horses? We need to check them, too."

"And we don't even know them," Stevie said. "They're not going to like this."

65

They walked back to the stable door and pushed it open. It gave a loud creak.

"Oh, no," Stevie whispered.

A light appeared on the boys' side of the loft, and A.J.'s red hair appeared at the window.

"What's going on?" he said.

Lisa, Carole, and Stevie were silent for a long moment.

"Nothing much," Lisa finally said.

"It must be something," A.J. said.

Stevie looked around quickly, desperate for an excuse. "We're . . . admiring the moonlight," she said. "It's so great!" Actually it was an ordinary half-moon.

"Hey, I love moonlight. I'll be right down," A.J. said.

The three girls looked at each other in dismay. "Of all people," Lisa said. A.J. was known for his chattiness—and his inquisitiveness.

Seconds later A.J. appeared in the doorway in a gray sweater. "This is fantastic," he whispered. "All my life I've been looking for people who are as crazy about moonlight as I am."

Stevie rolled her eyes.

"Just look at that ring around the moon," he said. "Isn't it fantastic?"

"Unbelievable," Lisa said.

"You can really see the seas on the moon," A.J. went on. "They're not real seas, of course. They're filled with dust. But they're called *mare*, which is Latin for 'sea.' "

Carole yawned.

"I guess the excitement of the moonlight has worn you out," A.J. said.

"It's a killer," Carole said. "Really draining."

"Have you guys made progress on the mystery?" he asked. "I'm not asking for clues or anything, just a general progress report."

Lisa let loose with a yawn so large her jaw ached. "You know what?" she said. "I think I've had enough moonlight."

"Me too," said Carole. "It's not good to have too much at one time."

"You guys are wimps," A.J. said cheerfully. "I'll be out here watching the moonlight for hours."

"Tell us about it in the morning," Stevie said as she stumbled toward the stairs.

"A.J.'s a little strange," Carole whispered as they crept up to the loft.

"And he's Phil's best friend," Stevie whispered. "It kind of makes you wonder."

As Stevie snuggled back into her sleeping bag, she

thought that her plan hadn't been a total success, but it hadn't been a total failure, either. They hadn't gotten a chance to check the guest horses, but at least they knew that none of the Pine Hollow horses was wearing barred shoes.

"PANDEMONIUM," LISA GROANED.

"What?" said Carole.

"Chaos," Lisa said. "I think I'll go back to sleep."

This, however, was not going to be possible. May, Amie, and Jackie were playing keep-away with a riding crop. The game involved a lot of jumping and shrieking. Corey was insisting that a thief had come during the night and stolen her toothbrush.

Lisa sat up, wishing—for only a second—that she was at home in her comfortable bed. But then she saw an amazing sight. Veronica was sitting at her portable dressing table staring at herself in the mirror. There was nothing unusual about this. Veronica spent half her life looking at herself in the mirror. But this morning she was staring at herself in dismay.

Veronica's hair gel seemed to have attracted every seed and bit of hay in the loft. Her rollers were coated with prickly tidbits.

"Veronica, you look like a giant thistle," said Stevie cheerfully. "And—to tell you the truth—the look suits you."

"It's not my fault," Veronica said crossly. "If only Pine Hollow had showers."

Corey and Amie were so amazed by Veronica's new look that they started dumping hay on each other's head, yelling, "We want to be beautiful like Veronica."

With a scornful toss of her head, Veronica picked up her brush, saying, "Some of my best ideas come out of problem situations."

"This I gotta see," said Stevie, crossing her arms.

Veronica slipped the rollers out of her hair and began to brush. But the seeds and hay bits had turned Veronica's hair gel into hair cement. As she brushed, her hair didn't flatten and fall. It stuck out at weird angles.

"Not even Frankenstein would marry you," said Corey. "In fact, he'd probably be *scared* of you."

Veronica's face turned pink. "This didn't happen by accident," she snapped. "It's somebody's fault. I heard people moving around last night." She glared at Lisa, Stevie, and Carole. "Somebody did this to me, and I think I know who."

The Saddle Club could hardly explain that they had gone downstairs to inspect horseshoes the night before, so they just shrugged.

The wake-up bell clanged. A minute later Deborah appeared at the head of the stairs. "Feed your horses, and then it will be time for breakfast," she said. Then she saw Veronica. She blinked hard.

"Are you all right, Veronica?" Deborah asked.

"Of course I'm all right," said Veronica, rising from her dressing table. "Or rather I would be if this dump had a shower."

Deborah nodded solemnly. "If only we did, Veronica. But I guess you're going to have to tough it out." She turned to the other riders. "Your horses are hungry. They're thirsty. Let's get going."

"Just like Max," Stevie grumbled. "Horse care first, people care second."

Lisa climbed out of her sleeping bag, rolled it up, and changed into her riding clothes. It felt funny to be getting dressed without taking a shower first—her mother would faint with horror if she knew—but it was fun. She went downstairs and waited in line at the bathroom until she got a chance to brush her teeth and give her face a quick wash.

She went to the feed room and forked hay off the end of a bale, filled a bucket with Max's special mixture of oats, sweet feed, and bran, and went to Prancer's stall.

"I hope we didn't wake you last night," she said to Prancer as she lifted the hay into her hay net. She started to explain to her why they'd had to check some of the other horses' shoes, but then Lisa realized that someone might be listening, so she just shrugged and said, "You know how it is." She poured the oat mixture into Prancer's feed bin and said, "Today is going to be really demanding. Think of yourself as a sleuth horse. That means a horse detective."

She filled Prancer's water bucket at the tap outside the stall and rehung it on the wall. Prancer was munching happily.

Lisa walked down the aisle and stood stretching at the open door. A misty morning fog covered the paddock in wisps and drifts. Behind it, the woods and hills rose like splashes of brilliant yellow and orange paint. Lisa sighed, thinking how beautiful it was.

On the edge of the woods there was a movement. *It must be a deer*, she thought, *because the deer in these woods are bold*. Sometimes at night they came out of the woods and ate whole flowerbeds.

As a puff of wind twirled the mist upward, Lisa strained to see. It wasn't a deer, it was a person on horseback. Lisa couldn't be sure, but it looked like a man. The horse was small and gray. The pair turned left. A bit of fog swept across the paddock, and the rider, who was a dark shadow now, edged his horse back toward the trees. Suddenly they bobbed over a jump and disappeared.

Lisa blinked. *That couldn't have been Nickel, could it?* she thought.

She turned and walked back down the aisle to Penny's stall. Inside, Lisa could hear Amie saying, "I'm not going to cry. I'm not. No way. Not me." Lisa looked over the stall door and saw that Amie had dropped Penny's fresh hay and was now trying to sweep it up in her arms, but she couldn't do it. The hay kept falling back to the floor.

"Can I come in?" Lisa said.

"If you like big messes," Amie said.

Lisa showed Amie how to start at one side of the dropped hay and curl it up like a jelly roll. The hay roll fit neatly in the hay net.

"Where did you learn that?" Amie asked.

"From Carole," Lisa said. "Not only does she know the big things about horse care, she knows the little ones, too."

73

"I'll never learn," Amie said.

"You've learned a lot already," Lisa said.

The two of them filled Penny's water bucket and walked down the aisle to see how Jackie was doing.

Red-faced and frustrated, Jackie was dragging Dime's water bucket down the aisle. She had filled it too full, and water had sloshed onto her breeches and her boots.

Lisa and Amie were stepping forward to help her when A.J. appeared.

"Heavy bucket?" he asked Jackie.

"No way," said Jackie bravely.

"You only need half that much water," A.J. said. He poured half out and gave the bucket back to Jackie.

"Hey," Jackie said. "I can do it now." Happily she carried the bucket into Dime's stall.

A.J. was a nice guy, Lisa thought. If only he didn't have that moonlight problem . . .

"Come on," A.J. said as he and Jackie left the stall. "I've heard this wild rumor that Max is making flapjacks."

Lisa and Amie grinned at each other.

"Max's Morning Madness," said Amie happily.

On an outdoor grill Max had set up a flat piece of iron. It was smoking.

"Your thing's on fire," Amie said.

"No, it's not," Max said. "And this thing is called a

griddle." With a flourish he poured a circle of batter on the griddle. The batter bubbled and then settled down to cook, sending off a nice steamy smell. Max poured a row of batter circles down the griddle, until there were ten. He stood back to look with satisfaction. When bubbles appeared in the center of the first flapjack, he flipped it. The underside was golden brown.

"Awesome," Amie said. "How do you know when to turn it?"

"When the bubbles in the center don't fill with wet batter," he said.

Max moved down the line flipping flapjacks. When he got to the end, he took a pile of paper plates and went back to the head of the line. He waited a minute and then neatly flipped the first flapjack onto a plate, adding a sausage from the frying pan on the other end of the grill.

"How do you know when the flapjack's done?" Amie said.

"When the edges curl," Max said.

"I wish I could do that," Amie said.

"It takes discipline, training, and respect for your materials," Max said. Everyone smiled because that was the way Max talked about riding.

Max's mother, who was affectionately known as Mrs.

Reg, circulated with forks, butter, syrup, and milk, while Deborah poured orange juice.

"What a breakfast," Stevie said, closing her eyes, savoring the slightly smoky flavor of the pancakes. "This should be called Max's Morning Magnificence."

"It's delicious," said Veronica, poking at her flapjack without really eating it.

"What's the matter, Veronica?" said A.J. "Worried about getting as fat as your hair?"

Veronica had managed to brush most of the seeds and hay out of her hair. She had even added a flippy curl at the bottom. The problem was that her hair was so stiff from all the gel, it stood out in a huge dome around her head.

"You may have to have your hair surgically removed," A.J. said.

"And then she'd be bald," Amie said.

For a second the MW riders imagined Veronica totally bald. Amie and Jackie gave each other high fives.

Fifteen minutes later everyone was groaning with satisfaction.

"I can't move," Peter said.

"I'll never eat again," Jasmine said. "Until lunch, that is."

Stevie turned to Lisa and said, "I can tell that Jasmine is

a true little sister of The Saddle Club. She can't wait for her next meal."

"Breakfast was so good I think Max deserves special thanks," Carole said.

"Thanks, Max," the riders called out.

"Not that kind of thanks," said Carole with a grin. "I think we should muck out the horses' stalls."

Everybody groaned. But they knew that Carole was right. First thing after breakfast, horses need to have their stalls cleaned.

"It would give Red a break and it would be a way of thanking Max for this great MW," Carole said.

As soon as the riders had stacked their plates and cups, they headed to the barn.

After Lisa took Prancer to the outdoor ring, she gave her stall a careful picking over. At first Lisa had really hated this part of horse care. But now she enjoyed it because Stevie had shown her a special way of moving the pitchfork in a swinging arc that made it feel lighter. When Lisa was done, she pushed the wheelbarrow out to the manure pile behind the barn and dumped it, then loaded it up with fresh wood chips. Lots of stables used straw for bedding, but Max said wood chips stayed dry longer. And, Lisa thought, they had a nice piney smell.

Lisa emptied the wood chips into the center of Prancer's stall and smoothed them with the back of her rake. At first this had driven her crazy, because just when she thought she had gotten the stall floor neat and flat, Max would point out that the sides were too high and the center was too low, and then she would have to start again. Stevie had shown her how to scrape down the sides and build up the center.

When Lisa was done, she led Prancer back to her stall. The horse nickered in appreciation. The best part of mucking out, Lisa thought, was that the horse really liked a clean stall.

As Lisa walked down the aisle, looking for Stevie and Carole, she passed the door to Nickel's stall. It looked empty and forlorn. Also, it needed cleaning. Sighing, Lisa went back for the wheelbarrow.

As she entered Nickel's stall, she thought how much like Nickel the stall was. The hay in the net had been neatly nibbled. The wood chips had been tidily pawed. Nickel was not a pony to make a mess or get overexcited, which was one of the things that made him so good for beginning riders.

But there was something odd on the door. Lisa stopped to look. It was a piece of red yarn. Another one! Why hadn't they seen it the day before? She would have to tell Stevie and Carole about this.

Then something else caught her eye—a spot of white on the hook where Nickel's feed bucket usually hung. It was a folded piece of paper. Lisa picked it off the hook and opened it. There was a poem inside. The poem didn't seem to make much sense, but Lisa knew it was a clue. This called for a meeting of The Saddle Club!

Casually Lisa strolled to Starlight's stall. Carole was giving the six-pointed star on his forehead a brushing.

Lisa whispered, "Come to Nickel's stall right away."

"No problem," Carole whispered.

"I'll get Stevie and meet you there," Lisa said.

Carole put down her brush and headed over to Nickel's stall at a slow walk, whistling as she went.

When Stevie and Lisa arrived, Carole noticed that Lisa's cheeks were pink with excitement.

"Listen to this," Lisa whispered, pulling the piece of paper out of her pocket.

East is east, and west is west
Whichever riders are the best
Will know there's only one place I could be.
Where once there grew a different type of tree
I've hidden your pony.

If you should want him back
You'll need no lack of bravery.
The way is hard, that's plain to see.
Water twice, and hills to climb
(I don't know how to rhyme this line!)

If Nickel isn't found by Sunday's light
(The strong light of day, not morning and not night)
I claim a forfeit, as is my right.
You'll owe your master, or D.C.,
A whole day's worth of misery.

"That's a big help," Stevie murmured.

Carole and Stevie read the paper again, and then read it a third time.

"It definitely means something," Stevie whispered. "I guess."

"I don't have a clue, but it definitely is a clue," said Carole with a giggle.

"A major clue," Stevie said.

"Maybe we should show it to the other riders," Carole said.

"Carole!" Stevie said. "First you have us mucking out the stalls, and now you want to give away our clue. I know it's important to be responsible, but let's not go overboard."

"Sorry," whispered Carole.

From down the aisle came Max's voice. "Riders who are done mucking can start tacking."

"We're going to be late," said Stevie.

"What should we do?" said Lisa.

"We have to leave the clue where we found it," Carole said.

Lisa knew this was true, so she put the poem back on the hook.

"Maybe we *should* tell the others," Carole whispered.

Stevie rolled her eyes.

From all around them came the sound of horses snorting as their riders began to tack them up.

"We've got to go. Otherwise we'll be the last out," Stevie said.

At that moment Stevie heard Starlight whinnying. Clearly the horse wanted to hit the trail.

"I guess we'd better go," Carole said.

"That's more like it," Stevie said. "Let's get a move on." She and Carole hurried out of Nickel's stall.

Lisa remembered that she hadn't had time to tell them about the mystery rider at the edge of the woods or the second piece of red yarn. Hurriedly Lisa finished cleaning

81

Nickel's stall and then went to saddle Prancer. This was all pretty confusing, she thought. Maybe MW stood for Mixed-up Weekend. Lisa lifted the saddle onto Prancer's back and fastened the girth.

"Lisa!" came Stevie's voice from the door of Prancer's stall.

Lisa looked up and saw that Stevie's hazel eyes were shining. "We're having an emergency meeting of The Saddle Club right now!" Stevie said. "Meet us in Nickel's stall immediately."

Two meetings of The Saddle Club in five minutes! It was all kind of nutty. Nonchalantly, so as not to attract attention, Lisa wandered back to Nickel's stall.

When she got there, Carole and Stevie were waiting.

"I've made a decision!" Stevie said dramatically. "I've thought things through and I know what The Saddle Club has to do."

Carole grinned. Stevie was great at figuring out reasons for doing exactly what she wanted. Undoubtedly Stevie was about to come across with the world's most ingenious reason for not telling about the note.

"It's not fair to the younger kids to hide the note," Stevie said. "They deserve a chance at solving the mystery. And if they haven't seen the note, what chance have they got?"

82

"I agree one hundred percent," said Carole. "But there is one drawback. If we tell them, Veronica will find out."

"That's just it," Stevie said triumphantly. "I *want* Veronica to find out. I don't want to beat her the easy way. I want her to know everything. Only then can we prove how truly dumb she is."

"Hmmm," Carole said. "I think this is a truly Stevian move. Now Veronica will have no excuses."

"That's it," Stevie said. "She will have to admit that The Saddle Club has brawn *and* brains."

"Good thinking," Carole said. But then she suddenly got cold feet. It was nice to be fair, but who wanted to be fair to Veronica?

"Maybe we should give this more thought," Carole said.

"After all, we found it," Lisa said.

"No," said Stevie heroically. "We are going to share this note with everyone. Anything less would be unworthy of The Saddle Club."

"It isn't easy being selfless," said Carole with a giggle.

"Anyway, we don't have to tell them about the bar-heeled shoe prints," said Stevie.

"This is true," Carole said.

"We don't have to tell them about this, either," said Lisa, pointing out the piece of red yarn. Chances were that when the other riders heard about the poem, they'd get so excited they'd forget to look for other clues.

The Saddle Club left Nickel's stall. As they walked down the aisle, they saw that most of the riders were nearly finished tacking up. From the snorts and pawing of the horses it was clear that they were ready to go.

Max was standing outside the tack room enjoying the hum of riders getting ready.

"Max, you've got to stop everything immediately!" said Stevie.

Max looked mildly skeptical. Stevie was always making pronouncements like this.

"We've found a major clue in Nickel's stall," Stevie said. "Everyone has to know."

"Call everyone," Lisa said.

"You really think I should?" Max said with a grin. "Everyone's eager to hit the trail."

"This is a must!" Stevie said grandly.

"Okay, if I have to," Max said. "Riders, assemble outside Nickel's stall."

There was a hush, then a stampede, as everyone rushed to see what was going on.

"I guess The Saddle Club had better explain," Max said.

"Look what we've found," said Lisa, pointing to the

sheet of paper in Nickel's stall. "It seems to be a sort of ransom note."

Max beamed and said, "You're kidding me."

"No," Lisa said. "It's a totally weird note, but it has to mean something."

"You're just trying to keep the really good detectives off the trail," said Veronica scornfully.

"So ignore it," said Stevie furiously.

"No," Max said. "The Saddle Club is doing something it doesn't have to. It's giving everyone an equal chance. I want you all to come to my office to listen to the contents of the note."

On the way to the office Max said to Lisa, "Since you're an experienced actress, I want you to read it."

9

With riders sitting on the floor staring up at her, Lisa lifted the paper and read the poem aloud.

When she was done, Lisa looked up. The riders were staring at her with open mouths.

"What's a D.C.?" Amie finally asked.

"The director of the Pony Club, silly," said Jackie. "In other words, Max."

"I knew that," said Amie, raising her chin. "I just wanted to see if you knew."

"That's the worst poem I ever heard," Veronica said.

"It is not," said Lisa indignantly. Having read the poem several times, she was starting to like it.

"Let me see that thing," said Veronica, standing up impatiently. Veronica's riding hat was perched on top of her stiff hair, making her look like a pinhead. This hadn't stopped her from trying to look gorgeous. She was wearing a new melton hunt jacket and a canary-yellow vest.

"It's time for a *real* detective to get to work," Veronica said as she took the note, spreading it out on Max's desk so that everyone could see it. "It's typed," she said, "so we can't analyze the handwriting."

"As if you're a handwriting analyst." A.J. smirked.

"For your information, I know quite a bit about hand-writing analysis," said Veronica airily. She tossed her head, something she often did, but this time her hair was mo-tionless and her riding hat jiggled.

"We could call the police and get them to dust it for fingerprints," said May.

"After The Saddle Club has smeared their greasy finger-prints all over it?" said Veronica. "I don't think so. In any case, what crime has been committed? Someone has writ-ten a perfectly dreadful poem, but that's not illegal."

At this, Max's expression became rather stiff, Stevie no-ticed.

"The real meaning is in the poem," Veronica said. "Some of us understand it, but some of us are too dim."

"Time to hit the trail," Max said, stepping forward. "Let the hunt begin."

As the riders broke into groups Max winked at Stevie, Carole, and Lisa. They could tell he was pleased that they'd shared their discovery of the note.

Jessica, Jackie, and Amie were giggling in the corner, saying something about red yarn.

"They found red yarn, too," said Lisa. "There seems to be a lot of it around."

"But what does it mean?" said Carole. "Yesterday we found yarn on the door of Nickel's stall. Today we found more. Amie, Jackie, and Jessica have found some, too. Where is all this yarn coming from?"

"Somewhere, somebody has part of a red sweater," Stevie said.

"The fact that we found red yarn yesterday and today means the thief has been here twice," Carole said.

"Why would the thief visit an empty stall?" Lisa asked.

"To leave the ransom note," said Stevie.

"Yes!" said Carole. "Let's take another look at that note."

They went over it line by line. " 'A different type of tree.' What's that?" said Stevie.

" 'Water twice and hills to climb,' " said Lisa. "The woods are full of hills and streams."

Carole groaned. "But which hills and streams?"

"It doesn't say anything about barred shoes," said Lisa sadly.

"It only makes the mystery more complicated," said Stevie, putting the note back on Max's desk. "Come on. We'd better saddle up. Everyone else is getting ready to go."

"Maybe the fresh air will clear our heads," Lisa said.

"Maybe," Stevie said doubtfully.

The tack room was empty because the other riders had already gotten their saddles.

"I'm looking forward to a nice brisk trot," said Lisa.

"Too bad we can't gallop," said Carole. "That would really clear our minds."

The gasp from Stevie was low, but filled with horror. "My saddle is gone."

THEY STARED AT the empty rack where the saddle had been.

"It's a trick," Stevie said. "And it's not funny."

"Why would it be a trick?" Carole asked.

"It's Max," Stevie said. "He must have sneaked in during breakfast."

"Would Max do that?" Lisa asked.

"Sure he would," Stevie said. "It's part of the mystery."

But Stevie wasn't as confident as she sounded. Would Max really steal her saddle as part of an MW? Somehow she didn't think he would do something that made her feel so terrible.

Then Stevie remembered May's tear-stained face the

day the MW began. She'd been so sure May's story about her saddle being stolen was part of the game. But later Judy Barker had told the Pony Clubbers that there was a tack thief on the loose—and now Stevie's saddle was missing.

Stevie shivered and shook her head, dismissing the terrible thought.

"If it's not Max, maybe it's A.J.," Stevie said. "I bet this is his idea of a joke."

"A.J. can be a little strange sometimes, but I can't see him doing anything this mean," Carole said.

"Well, who did, then?" asked Stevie.

Lisa and Carole shrugged helplessly.

"We'd better tell Max," Carole said. "He needs to know."

"If he doesn't already," Stevie said glumly. The Saddle Club headed off to look for him. They found Max outside, watching Mystery Teams ride off in all directions.

"My saddle's gone," Stevie said miserably.

Max's blue eyes flashed. "I'm calling the police," he said. "Officer Kent will want to know." Max was silent for a minute, then he spoke up again. "Stevie, find yourself another saddle and hit the trail. I don't want your weekend ruined." He spun on his heel and headed briskly toward his office.

"Come on," Lisa said. "Let's go." They ran back to the tack room.

Carole grabbed Starlight's saddle from its rack and his bridle from its hook. Lisa got Prancer's tack. Stevie hesitated and then took Topside's saddle. Topside wasn't being ridden on the Mystery Weekend, so he wouldn't need it.

Stevie took the saddle to Belle's stall. It was too broad for the mare, so she returned to the tack room for an extra saddle pad. Stevie finished saddling Belle and set off to meet Lisa and Carole at the good-luck horseshoe.

"If we ever needed luck, we need it today," Lisa said.

Stevie touched the horseshoe twice.

"How is Topside's saddle on Belle?" Lisa asked.

"Belle's not comfortable," Stevie said. "She knows it's the wrong saddle." In fact, Belle was twitching her coat and looking cross.

Carole gave Stevie a sympathetic look. "There's nothing worse than putting the wrong saddle on a horse."

"It's like wearing someone else's riding boots," Stevie said.

Carole looked down at her own riding boots, which were scuffed and scarred. Somehow she never had to worry about anyone else wearing her boots.

"Hey," Carole said, staring at the ground next to her foot. "Look at that."

Beside the doorway was the fresh print of a bar-heeled shoe.

Stevie jumped down from Belle to look. She touched the rim. "It's fresh," she said. "It's wet." She looked toward the woods. "Max's thief must have just been here." She climbed back on Belle. "Let's go."

"I forgot to tell you," Lisa said, clapping her hand to her forehead. "There's been so much going on. When I was out here before breakfast I saw someone riding in the mist. Over there." She pointed to the two maple trees where the rider had disappeared. "It was someone on a gray horse. The horse was small. It could have been a large pony. For all I know, it could have been Nickel."

"He would have gone into the woods at the first available spot," said Carole.

"There!" Stevie said, pointing to a wooden coop jump.

"Stevie!" Carole said. "You know that pasture. It has barbed wire all around it. The people who own the pasture don't want riders to use it."

Stevie walked Belle over to the jump. Sure enough, the pasture was totally fenced in.

"Look at this," said Lisa with a grin.

Stevie wondered how Lisa could be smiling at a time like this. But when she looked down she saw that there was a set of bar-heeled prints leading to the jump. And then another set leading away on the same side.

"The thief jumped in, saw he was stuck, and jumped back out," Lisa said. "This gives us catch-up time. It means he can't be far ahead."

"Great," said Stevie grimly. "When we catch him, that prankster is going to get a piece of my mind."

"Look," Carole said. The dark bar-heeled prints led toward a trail that edged the woods.

"Excellent," said Lisa, pressing her knees to Prancer's flanks, encouraging her to trot.

Carole shook her shoulders, getting rid of the cricks that came from sleeping on the floor of the loft.

The trail ran into the forest.

"This is where we heard the hoofbeats on Thursday," Lisa pointed out. "We were almost back to the barn when we heard those clops—the ones Stevie thought belonged to a jackrabbit."

Stevie wondered if the mysterious hoofbeats had anything to do with the bar-heeled shoe prints they were following. But they couldn't have, she thought, because the girls had heard the hoofbeats on Thursday, and the Mystery Weekend hadn't begun yet. A spiderweb caught Stevie across the forehead, and she peeled it loose.

Truly, Stevie thought, it wasn't easy to follow hoofprints

94

and trot at the same time. It was kind of like a competition event. Stevie leaned against Belle's neck to avoid a low-hanging branch. "Branch," she yelled as she pushed it out of her way.

Lisa saw the branch bob back in front of her. If she didn't do something, it would knock her off Prancer's back. "Whoa!" she yelled. She pulled on the reins and sank her weight into her heels. This was what Max called an emergency stop.

Prancer dug in her hooves and came to a halt.

"Yikes," yelled Carole, pulling up Starlight behind her.

"It's like a freeway pileup," said Lisa.

"It's a good thing I just had Starlight's brakes tuned," Carole said with a laugh.

"You're telling me," said Lisa, whose heart was still pounding. She looked at the threatening branch. It was naked except for a spot of red at the tip. Something about that red was familiar. Lisa reached up and pulled the branch toward her. It was a piece of red yarn. "Look!" She held it high so that Stevie and Carole could see, and then she put it back on the branch.

"We know we're on the right trail now," said Lisa.

Stevie turned back to the path. "You trot, I'll look for clues," she said to Belle. "Soon we'll have that saddle back. I miss it just as much as you do."

There were bar prints around the edge of a puddle. Then prints crushed into moist grass. Then a wet bar print on a fallen pale maple leaf.

"I saw two more pieces of yarn," Lisa called.

There was a patch of gray sky ahead, and suddenly Stevie and Belle were trotting across an upland meadow filled with wiry silver grass. Stevie could feel Belle wanting to gallop, but Max had forbidden it.

At the other side of the meadow was a rider on a small gray horse. The rider was a blur of blue.

"There," Stevie called back to Lisa and Carole. "On the other side of the field."

When Stevie looked ahead again, the gray horse was jumping a fallen log. And then horse and rider disappeared.

"Let's go," Stevie said. She pressed her knees against the mare's sides and put her heels down. Belle took off in a swift canter, her hooves pounding the ground. Stevie knew they'd catch the thief soon, because there was no way an ordinary horse could outrun Belle.

Stevie could see the log the gray horse had jumped. She urged Belle toward it. Belle's stride lengthened and lightened.

They were sailing across the log when she saw the man

on the gray horse crashing down the trail ahead of her. He disappeared into a stand of hemlock trees.

Lisa and Prancer came flying over the log, followed by Carole and Starlight.

"He's just ahead," Stevie said. "In the trees."

They trotted to the edge of the trees and saw the man at the far side of the grove. He must have heard them, because he urged the gray horse into a gallop.

"We can't let him get away," Stevie said. "Let's gallop."

Trotting beside her, Lisa shook her head. "Prancer might go crazy," she said. Prancer was an ex-racehorse. Lisa had never ridden her all out, and she had promised Max that she wouldn't until he gave her permission.

Stevie looked at Carole. But Carole shook her head. "Horse honor," she shouted. Her words seemed to get lost in the trees.

"My saddle," Stevie groaned, but she knew Carole was right.

Stevie, Lisa, and Carole trotted out of the hemlock grove, past a creek bed filled with rocks, and up a rise where the trail turned slippery and treacherous. They slowed to a walk. At the top of the rise they looked at a winding upland trail. The ground was dry, so there were no tracks. Up ahead was a fork in the trail.

"No tracks," said Stevie forlornly. She wished that they had taken a chance and galloped.

"I haven't seen any yarn in a while," said Lisa.

"We'll just have to guess," said Carole. She was feeling guilty, wondering if maybe it would have been all right if they had galloped a bit.

"Let's go left," said Stevie without conviction.

Listlessly the horses turned left. They could tell that their riders were discouraged. Belle looked over her shoulder, back toward Pine Hollow, and Stevie knew that she was thinking about an afternoon nap.

"I just thought of something," Stevie said. When Lisa and Carole turned, they saw that Stevie was pale.

"The rider wasn't wearing red." Stevie realized that her worst fears had come true. Her saddle was gone, and the person who had taken it wasn't playing by the rules of the game.

11

"CHEER UP," AMIE said to Stevie. "If you keep trying, you're bound to make progress with the mystery."

Great, Stevie thought, *I'm being given advice by a little kid.* But she knew that Amie meant well, so she said, "Thanks, Amie. I appreciate your concern."

Amie patted Stevie on the shoulder and said, "Don't feel bad."

Stevie felt terrible. She and Lisa and Carole had totally lost the trail, and then the lunch bell rang. Now she felt as if she'd never see her saddle again.

Mrs. Reg passed Stevie a cup of chili. "It's my five-alarm chili," Mrs. Reg said.

Stevie looked at the chili with concern. She didn't like fiery food.

"Minus four alarms," Mrs. Reg said with a smile. "In other words, this is one-alarm chili."

"That's what I like," Stevie said. She slid the relish tray toward her so she could add cheddar cheese chunks, cucumber slices, bits of onion, and sour cream. Now that she thought of it, the crumbled egg looked good, too. And then she added some lettuce strips. And bacon bits. "Is this all?" she asked.

"I ran out of snails," said Mrs. Reg with a laugh.

At the mention of snails a large "yeeeeeew" went up from the riders.

"But I have some octopus in the refrigerator," Mrs. Reg said.

"That's okay," Stevie said. "Let's save the octopus for our midnight snack." She went back to the rock where Carole and Lisa were sitting.

"What a bummer," Lisa said. Lisa was usually so neat, but now her wavy light brown hair was escaping from her ponytail, she'd gotten a smudge on her forehead, and there was a streak of mud on the knee of her breeches. All three of them were tired and frustrated, and so were their horses.

"We have to think," Lisa said. "There must be a solution to this problem."

100

"I've decided to give up thinking," Stevie said. "It just makes me feel worse."

"The way I see it is this," said Lisa, keeping her voice low so that the other riders couldn't hear. "If the rider we saw was the one who stole Nickel, then he should have been wearing red. That red yarn has got to be one of Max's clues. A rider might snag his sweater in a horse stall, but no one leaves piece after piece of yarn in trees."

"It's just like Max to plant a lot of clues to make sure the younger riders don't miss out," Stevie said.

"That's just what I was thinking," Carole said.

"So why wasn't the rider we saw wearing red?" Lisa asked. She looked carefully from Stevie to Carole, wondering if they were thinking what she was thinking.

"It's creepy," Stevie said softly.

"It's crawly," said Carole.

But Lisa had to keep going to the end of her thought. "The man who was riding away from us was a real thief, not a pretend thief. He's not part of the Mystery Weekend."

"So if he's a real thief, and not Max's thief . . . ," Carole said slowly.

Stevie turned pale. "It means all of my suspicions were right. My saddle was really stolen."

"How can a man on horseback steal a saddle?" Carole said practically. "There's no way he could carry it."

Lisa's eyes grew large. "That's easy," she whispered. "He took the saddle this morning, right before I saw him riding away."

"He rode up bareback, stole my saddle, and rode away on it," said Stevie.

"It's so simple," said Lisa softly. "The woods around here are filled with trails and bridle paths. It'd be so easy for him to disappear."

"Those hoofbeats we heard on Thursday were probably him," Carole said.

"He was casing Pine Hollow. He was figuring out how to rob it," Stevie said.

They shivered.

"If someone sees a rider on the trail, they don't think anything of it," Carole said.

"That's right," Stevie said thoughtfully. "These woods are part of the state park. Anyone can ride in them."

"It's kind of brilliant, when you think of it," said Lisa.

"*Too* brilliant, if you ask me," Stevie said. "What kind of lunkheaded thief would ride a horse that leaves bar-heeled shoe prints all over the trails? Or steal a saddle from a stable that just happens to be jam-packed with kids?"

"You mean you think there's more than one mystery in this MW?" asked Carole.

"That's exactly what I think," said Stevie. "Max is even more devious than we imagined." *At least I hope he is*, she added silently to herself.

Stevie looked into her cup of chili. Somehow, during this totally upsetting conversation, she had eaten it all. She went and got another helping and came back.

"I want my saddle back *now*—not tomorrow afternoon," Stevie said miserably.

"Don't worry," Lisa said firmly. "And after lunch we're going to go back and find the thief."

After lunch, and after their horses had a chance to rest, they set off on the trail again, but this time they were quiet and thoughtful.

The sky had changed. Now it was gray and flat, with hawks skimming low under the clouds. It was as if winter were just over the horizon.

When they got back to the fork where they'd lost the thief, they sat on their horses trying to decide where to go.

"Which way?" said Lisa, looking from one branch of the trail to the other.

"You know," said Carole suddenly, "I think I remember where we are. This isn't a fork, really—it's a loop. It goes back to the edge of a county road, follows it for a while, and then circles back. So we don't have to make a choice."

"We still have to pick one way," Lisa pointed out.

Carole nodded to the right fork. "That way you have to cross the stream again and go through an apple orchard. It's a long way to the road. This way," she went on, pointing to the left, "you come to the road more quickly, and I think there's an empty farmhouse with a barn."

"A farmhouse!" Stevie said. "Maybe that's where the thief is hiding out."

"Let's hope," Lisa said with a quaver in her voice.

The three looked at one another. For the first time it struck them that they could be chasing someone who was dangerous.

"We have to be quiet."

"Like mice," Stevie agreed, "except quieter. That's not easy for horses." She looked at Carole, who was the best rider.

Carole took the lead, wondering if she was up to this. She knew how to get Starlight over a jump, and how to do a counter-canter, and how to pirouette to the right. But how do you get a horse to be quiet?

Carole made her hands light and her seat light. Starlight took a couple of prancing steps, which sent up a spray of gravel. "Easy," Carole whispered. "Walk softly." Somehow

Starlight got the idea. He advanced forward with slow, delicate steps. Behind her, Carole heard Prancer and Belle slip into the same delicate rhythm.

The landmarks on the trail passed slowly. First there was a stand of lady's slippers with pulpy yellow stems and delicate red flowers. And then there was a fallen log with wedges of white fungus.

The path disappeared around a grove of white birches. Carole listened to Starlight's breathing. It was peaceful, almost sleepy. As Starlight rounded the birch trees Carole saw a weather-beaten house and barn just beyond the edge of the woods.

Carole raised her hand for Lisa and Stevie to stop. They had to find cover so they could observe the barn. There was a bunch of giant rhododendron bushes with long, leathery leaves to the right. The normal thing would have been to circle into it, but Carole couldn't do that. It would have been too obvious. She had to get Starlight to back into the bushes.

Horses don't like to move backward. They especially don't like to back into things like bushes. Carole pulled gently on Starlight's reins. Starlight stepped back, using the same soft tread. When the rhododendron leaves brushed his flanks, he shivered.

"Easy, easy," Carole whispered.

Starlight stepped tentatively backward, and the leaves parted. In four steps he was safe in the center of the bushes.

"You're great," Carole whispered, reaching down to stroke his neck.

Prancer was shaking her head from side to side. The idea of creeping backward into a stand of bushes was not something that appealed to the former racehorse.

Lisa rubbed Prancer's neck. She was the most complicated and special horse she'd ever ridden. "You can do it," she whispered.

Lisa pulled gently on Prancer's reins. Prancer moved into the bushes like a champion.

"Now you," Stevie whispered to Belle. "If they can do it, you can." Belle was stubborn. She loved games, but she also loved to have her own way. She pawed at the soft earth, but then she relaxed and stepped back into the bushes, too.

"I know where we are," Lisa whispered. "I've seen this house from the road. I know which road it is, too."

"Good," Stevie whispered.

"There's a car in front of the house," Carole whispered. "So there's probably someone home."

"If he isn't out stealing saddles," said Stevie bitterly.

A few minutes later they heard it—the sound of someone whistling, a cheery sound. Stevie tried to identify the tune and realized that it was "Oh! Susannah."

A man appeared with his hands in the pockets of a blue hacking jacket. He went into the ramshackle barn and came back in a moment, leading a bridled gray horse.

The man sprang lightly up onto the horse's bare back, and headed . . .

. . . straight toward The Saddle Club!

12

LISA, STEVIE, AND Carole couldn't move. They couldn't speak. They looked at each other, their eyes full of terror. But at the last minute the rider veered left and headed into the woods.

"That was close," Stevie whispered.

"What happens when you faint on horseback?" Lisa said.

"Your nose winds up in the horse's mane," Carole said.

"Let's go search the barn," Stevie said. "It's bound to be full of clues. And maybe even my saddle."

Lisa didn't agree. "If your saddle's there now, it'll be

there later. I bet that thief is on his way to steal another saddle. We have to stop him."

Reluctantly Stevie looked at the barn. She wanted her saddle. She wanted to put it on Belle's back. But she knew that Lisa was right. A crime was almost certainly about to be committed, and it was up to The Saddle Club to stop it.

They turned onto the trail.

"Look," said Stevie grimly. She pointed to hoofprints on the ground. The gray horse was wearing bar-heeled shoes!

"Full speed ahead," said Stevie. But then, not quite sure that this was a good idea, she turned to Carole and said, "Right?"

Even at such a serious moment Carole had to smile. Stevie was so filled with contradictions.

"The trail is clear, so we don't have to worry about losing it," Carole said. "And the ground is soft, so the horses won't make much noise. And the wind is blowing back toward us, so we can hear the thief, but he can't hear us. So, yes, full speed ahead!"

Stevie urged Belle to trot. She lengthened the reins to give Belle headroom and felt the mare's pace lengthen, her steps beginning to glide.

Ahead Stevie could hear the faint clop of hooves. Through the trees came a whinny. It was high-pitched, excited-sounding.

Over her shoulder Stevie said, "Something's happened. Let's go." She pressed her heels down, getting ready to give Belle the signal to gallop.

"What if he sees us?" Lisa whispered.

Over her shoulder Stevie gave her a fierce look. "This time I'm galloping," she said. "I'm catching up to him."

Belle took off, her feet pounding into the soft earth, sending up bits of leaves and grass. Carole, riding behind her, had to duck to avoid the spray.

Up ahead was a turn in the road. "Faster," said Stevie. Belle stretched her legs, running in a smooth, even gait that showed her championship style.

Stevie braced herself as they went into the turn. It was like a racetrack, she thought. They were about to enter the homestretch.

Belle rounded the corner. Ahead, the gray horse was trying to escape into the woods. The thief was yanking the reins and struggling as the horse whinnied shrilly.

What was making the gray horse so crazy? To the left the woods thinned. Beyond that was a small apple orchard with very old, neglected, half-dead trees. On the other side of the orchard, an abandoned shed sat in the middle of a clearing. From behind the shed came a whinny.

The gray horse plunged and bucked, trying to head toward the shed. His rider leaned back, sawing cruelly on the reins. The horse reared, his front legs pawing the air. Panicked, the rider leaned forward and pounded the horse's neck. That did it. The gray horse crashed into the woods, toward the orchard.

Carole and Lisa came cantering around the corner and pulled up next to Stevie.

"Where'd he go?" Lisa said.

"He's lost control of his horse," Stevie said. "He's crashing around in the woods somewhere. No way am I going after him. Belle could get hurt."

"It's good to see you can think of your horse at a moment like this," Carole said. But then she got a funny look on her face. "You know, I have the feeling this place has something to do with the ransom poem. 'Where once there grew a different kind of tree, I've hidden your pony,'" she recited.

"What?" Stevie said.

"When you plant an orchard, you have to cut down forest trees," Lisa said thoughtfully.

"So here there used to be a different kind of tree," said Stevie.

"And if we'd come from the other direction, we could have crossed the creek again. That's 'water twice,'" Carole said.

"Maybe the riddle does make sense," Stevie said.

From behind the shed came a loud whinny.

"That's Nickel," Lisa said, her eyes widening. "I'd know his whinny anywhere."

"Looks like we solved the riddle," Stevie said with a grin. "I guess the best team won."

Suddenly, from the far side of the clearing, they heard a commotion on the trail. The wind carried the distant sound of shrieking and giggling to The Saddle Club.

Jackie, Amie, and Jessica appeared, followed by Max.

"It's Max," Stevie said to Carole and Lisa. "Let's go tell him what we found." Carole and Lisa nodded, and the three hurried their horses through the thin woods. As they neared the orchard they could hear the younger riders chattering.

"We win!" Amie said. "We solved the mystery. Right, Max? Right? There's Nickel. We followed the red yarn and now we're here."

"It seems you're right," said Max.

"We're champions," said Jessica. "We're number one."

A young man walked out from behind the shed, leading Nickel. It was Phil!

Stevie's jaw dropped open, and she pulled Belle to a halt. Carole and Lisa stopped next to her.

"That sneak," Stevie whispered. "That liar, that creep. He's been here all weekend. His grandmother wasn't even sick. And I fell for it hook, line, and sinker. I don't want him to see me here. He'll laugh himself sick."

Lisa and Carole looked at Stevie with sympathy. First her saddle was stolen, and now this.

Phil was wearing a bright red sweater—and it had only one arm!

"Phil," cried Amie delightedly. "You're the crook."

"None other," said Phil, bowing. "You caught me red-handed."

"And red-sweatered," said Jackie.

Suddenly, Stevie remembered the familiar figure in red she had spotted at Pine Hollow on the first morning of the MW. It must have been Phil slinking around, she thought, groaning. She watched as Phil waved to Max.

"I guess Nickel could use some attention," Max said to Amie, Jackie, and Jessica. "Although Phil's been taking good care of him, I bet he's feeling kind of lonely."

"As a matter of fact, I just happen to have a carrot for Nickel," said Amie.

"And I have an apple," said Jackie.

"And I have a knock-knock joke," said Jessica. As a little sister of The Saddle Club, she was crazy about knock-knock jokes.

The girls gathered around the pony. Meanwhile Max

and Phil led the other horses to the far side of the orchard, where there was a succulent patch of green grass.

"Okay, Nickel," said Jessica. "I've got a really good one for you. Knock, knock."

"Who's there?" said Amie, talking for Nickel.

"Sam and Planet," Jessica said.

The Saddle Club shook their heads. Jessica had the joke totally wrong.

"Sam and Planet who?" said Amie.

"Someone planted stinkweed," Jessica sang in a loud voice. "In Redford O'Malley's riding boots."

Amie, Jackie, and Jessica collapsed in laughter.

"That's the worst knock-knock joke I ever heard," Carole whispered.

But Lisa gasped with fright. "Look," she whispered.

The gray horse was barreling out of the woods toward the orchard and the clearing on the other side, where the little girls were standing. The horse's eyes were rolling, and his face was flecked with foam. The rider clung desperately to the horse's mane.

"We've got to warn them," Carole said.

"Amie," Stevie yelled.

But the wind carried her words away.

"Come on," Stevie said. She shook the reins, pressed her knees tightly to Belle's sides, and yelled, "Go." No time for subtlety now. Belle headed into the orchard, straight at the gray horse. "Keep going," Stevie said. "Please!"

Horses hate to run into other horses, and Stevie was afraid that Belle would veer off. But Belle barreled toward the gray horse, with Starlight and Prancer close behind.

The gray horse shied, nearly throwing his rider. Snorting and spraying flecks of foam, the horse careened back into the woods.

The little girls weren't aware of the drama that had just unfolded on the other side of the orchard.

"After him!" Stevie cried. This seemed to be all Belle needed. She headed into the woods.

"Go," Lisa said, steering Prancer after them.

"Yes!" said Carole as Starlight took off.

Stevie ducked under a branch. There was a huge fallen tree up ahead. They'd have to go around it somehow. But Belle rose gracefully in a jump. The only problem was that she seemed to be rising directly into a hemlock tree. "Yikes," Stevie cried. But Belle knew what she was doing. They missed the tree by a hair. Stevie let out a yell of triumph as Belle landed on the edge of an inky puddle, splashing Carole.

Carole couldn't see. She had a funny taste in her mouth. For a moment she couldn't figure out what had happened.

Then she realized she'd been mudded. She wiped the mud from her eyes and let out a whoop.

Lisa had her knees tight and her heels down. She was trying not to think about what was going on. She wasn't ready for this kind of wild cross-country riding.

Stevie heard an anguished cry and a splash up ahead. She zoomed around the corner and pulled Belle to a stop.

The gray horse was still racing wildly, but his rider had been thrown. The thief had fallen in the creek and was yelling with pain.

Coming up behind Stevie, Carole swerved and stopped. Lisa nearly crashed into them.

The gray horse scrambled frantically up the shallow creek bed.

This was terrible, Lisa knew. A frightened horse running over slippery rocks could break a leg. Someone had to catch him . . . and she had the fastest horse.

Lisa took a deep breath and headed Prancer toward the creek, looking for secure footing. Daintily Prancer picked her way through the stones and leaped onto the other bank. There was a narrow path along the edge of the bank. Would it hold them? There was no choice. It was the only way to follow the gray horse.

"Easy," she said to Prancer. "Nothing sudden."

Prancer looked at the trail and snorted. Most horses shy

116

from narrow passages, but Prancer bobbed her head and started along the path, stepping evenly. Beneath her feet pebbles showered into the stream, but Prancer didn't panic.

The path ended abruptly. The land dropped sharply downhill.

Desperately Lisa looked around. The other side of the creek was safer, the ground more solid, but it was far away. "Can you jump?" she said to Prancer. "I know it's far."

Lisa knew that standing jumps are difficult for horses. Usually they won't make them. But Prancer sprang lightly across the creek onto the other side. Just as she did the gray horse bolted out of the creek bed and headed for a stand of pines.

"Go," Lisa said to Prancer. She put her hands low and bent over Prancer's neck, feeling the power of the horse's muscular chest. Prancer ran through the pine forest, gathering speed. For Lisa, it was like being on a rocket.

They were on the edge of a field of winter grass. The gray horse streaked forward, trailing flecks of foam. Lisa knew she had to catch him before he disappeared into the trees on the other side of the field.

She put her hand on Prancer's withers. She didn't have to say anything or make any motion. The horse knew. Looking at the broad expanse of field, Lisa felt frightened.

It seemed so far. But she knew that Max would want her to catch the gray horse. She took a deep breath.

At first she could feel the thumping of hoofbeats in her chest and arms. But as Prancer's stride lengthened the thumping stopped. It seemed like everything else was moving, and they were standing still. For a second Lisa felt almost as if Prancer might lift off the ground and fly.

Head down, the gray horse streaked toward the woods. Prancer was already running full out. But she would have to go faster.

Please, Lisa thought. *You can do it. You're a champion.*

Prancer gathered herself—Lisa could feel the concentration—and lengthened her stride, head down, mane flying.

The trees on the edge of the field were approaching fast, too fast. The little gray horse was almost there.

Lisa gasped. Suddenly they were next to the gray horse, but they were also moving too fast for Lisa to catch the horse's reins.

Prancer seemed to understand perfectly. She slowed alongside the other horse, and the gray slowed slightly, too.

Lisa reached out and grabbed the reins. "Easy, easy," she said, but the gray horse whinnied and kept running.

Prancer snorted. It was just an everyday snort—a humdrum kind of snort. Suddenly Lisa realized that she could count on Prancer and that everything was going to be okay. "Cool it," she said firmly to the gray horse. The horse shivered and settled into a trot, then a walk.

Lisa's hands were shaking, but now she had control. She turned to the gray horse and said, "Are you okay?"

The horse gave her a sideways look. Lisa could have sworn he looked grateful to have his flight end.

"Come on," Lisa said. She turned Prancer, and they headed into a trot. It wasn't good to walk after a run like that. Both horses needed to be cooled down or they would cramp.

In a minute the gray horse was moving calmly next to Prancer. The mare trotted proudly with her head up and her knees rising smartly. Lisa smiled, thinking that she would have to tell Max that Prancer had run all out and that she had been able to handle it. From now on maybe Max would trust her with more challenging rides.

MEANWHILE, CAROLE AND Stevie were trying to figure out what to do with the thief.

He was sitting in the cold creek complaining bitterly. "I want out of here right now," he said. "And that means instantly."

"So you can steal more saddles?" Stevie said. "I don't think so."

"All right, all right," the thief said. "So I took a couple of saddles. That doesn't mean I have to freeze to death with a busted leg."

"Stay right there," Carole said.

"What do you think I'm doing?" the thief said. "Does it look like I'm running around?"

"We'd better tie him up," Stevie said.

"That's it," Carole agreed.

But they didn't have any rope.

"I read about how the Indians made rope out of bark," Stevie said. "Maybe we could do that."

They looked at the trees that lined the creek bed. Somehow making rope seemed like a long-term project. They needed to tie up the thief right away.

"I took a basket-weaving course once," Carole said. "And they said that vines have incredible strength."

"Basket-weaving!" moaned the thief. "I've been brought down by a couple of hobbyists."

There was a tangle of vines next to the creek. Carole pulled them out by the roots and walked gingerly toward the thief.

"Reach for the sky," Carole said.

"Reach for the sky yourself," he sneered.

In action movies it was never like this, Stevie thought.

120

Carole held out the vines. They looked about as strong as limp spaghetti.

"Will you two bimbos get me out of here?" said the thief. "I'm freezing. My leg feels funny." His stern mouth grimaced. "I'm injured."

Stevie and Carole were always ready to help someone who needed it. But how did they know he was telling the truth?

"How exactly does your leg feel?" asked Carole. She knew a little about first aid from her work as a vet's apprentice to Judy Barker.

"It feels great," the thief said bitterly.

Carole stepped over to look. The thief's right leg was at an impossible angle. She could see that it was broken.

"We'd better get him out of the creek," Carole said to Stevie. "He could go into shock. If he goes into shock, he'll turn pale and break out into a sweat, and his blood pressure will go way down. Shock is very dangerous. He could die from it."

Now the thief really was pale.

"We don't want him to die under our noses," Stevie said.

They waded into the creek.

"We should use a balanced lift here," Carole said. "If we don't, he could fall and, if his leg is broken, that could drive bits of bone into a nerve, and if the nerve is severed, the leg could become paralyzed for life. At least, I think so."

"I don't feel so hot," the thief muttered. He was no longer pale. He was green.

"On the other hand, if his spinal cord is broken, and we lift him, that could be *really* dangerous—his whole body might become paralyzed," Carole said. "But I don't think we should leave him in this frigid water. It's sort of a fifty-fifty thing."

"Please move me," said the thief in a timid voice. "I'll do anything."

Stevie knelt down, holding the thief's left arm. Carole knelt down, taking his right.

"Easy," he groaned.

"Breathe deeply," Carole said. "Try to relax."

"Yeah, right," he muttered. But Stevie could see that he was trying. He was taking long, slow breaths.

"Can you stand on your good leg?" Carole said.

The thief pushed his left foot close to his body, and Stevie and Carole lifted him.

"Careful," he whispered.

They helped him hop to the bank and then eased him onto the grass.

The thief closed his eyes and leaned back, sweat pouring

down his face. He opened his eyes, wiped his forehead, and said, "I'm not going to die, am I?"

"The next half hour is crucial," Carole said. "If we get help right away, you might make it."

"But I don't think it looks good," Stevie said. "It'll take us more than a half hour to ride for help. And I'm riding slower than usual these days since I'm using a borrowed saddle." She narrowed her eyes meaningfully at the thief, but by now his eyes were closed again.

Above them they heard the sound of hooves. They looked up. Lisa was on Prancer.

"Where've you been?" said Stevie.

"I went to catch the gray horse," Lisa said. "The way he was running, I was afraid he'd injure himself. And then I went back to the orchard, found Max and Phil, and told them what happened."

Just then Max and Phil appeared on horseback.

"We got him," Stevie said triumphantly.

Phil grinned. "I thought I was going to be the big surprise of this weekend, but once again the big surprise is The Saddle Club."

"What can we do?" said Stevie modestly. "We just stumble into things."

"Hey, guys!" said the thief. "What about me?"

"Have you got any dying requests?" Stevie asked.

"Yes," croaked the thief. "Call the police. *Please*."

Phil reached into his saddlebag and whipped out a cellular phone.

Stevie stared at it with wonder. "Where'd you get that?"

"Max gave it to me for emergencies," Phil said. With a dramatic gesture he handed the phone to Stevie. "Since you guys caught the real thief, I think you're the ones who should call the police." He looked over at Max, who nodded.

Stevie punched 911.

"I'd like to report that a crime has been solved," Stevie said into the phone. "No, we don't need help. The varmint has been caught and wants to confess. Go to County Route 11, pass the intersection with Route 46, and turn left. You'll find a fire road with a gate." Stevie listened. "That's right, a gate," she said. "Be sure you open it toward your car, or you'll damage the hinges. And don't forget to shut it afterward. Once you're in the pasture . . ."

By the time Stevie finished, everyone except the thief was laughing.

13

"I CAN'T BELIEVE Max is paying for this," Stevie said as she licked the marshmallow, fudge sauce, peanut butter, and lime sherbet from her spoon.

The girls were at TD's, the local ice cream parlor, a few days later.

"If he saw what you were eating, he probably wouldn't believe it either," said Lisa as she watched Stevie swallow the weird concoction.

"That's a dull one—for her," said the waitress. "I'd say that one is practically normal—*for her*."

"Normal!" said Stevie, looking at the sundae in horror. She looked up at Lisa and Carole. "Tell me it's not normal."

"It's not normal," said Lisa and Carole together. The waitress stomped off.

Stevie licked her spoon and said, "You know what the truth is?"

"What?" said Lisa.

"We don't deserve these sundaes," said Stevie dramatically.

"How come?" said Carole.

"Max is thanking us for letting Jessica, Jackie, and Amie take credit for solving the pretend mystery," Stevie said. "The thing is, they *did* solve it. They followed the red yarn to the apple orchard. They spotted Nickel. They won the prize fair and square."

"Hmmm," Carole said. "I believe you're right."

"We found Nickel totally by accident," Stevie said. "We didn't follow the red yarn clues. We were following the barred shoe prints, which had nothing to do with the pretend mystery."

"On the other hand, we did solve an actual crime," Lisa said.

"There's that," Stevie agreed.

"And the thief won't be stealing saddles in the near future."

"Or ever again," Stevie said. "Officer Kent told Max

that the thief said he's going to do something nice and safe from now on, like mop floors."

"That's after he gets out of prison—if he goes to prison," Lisa said.

"He was a terrible horseman," Carole said. "Did you see the way he jerked that horse's reins?"

"Disgusting," Lisa said. "Max is going to find a good home for the gray horse."

Max had said that he couldn't keep the gray horse at Pine Hollow because of its soft hooves. A stable horse had to have strong feet. But the gray horse would do well on a farm with only one rider.

Stevie sighed happily and said, "I will never, never forget Veronica's expression when she found out that she hadn't solved either the pretend mystery or the real mystery."

"She was so upset, she spilled spaghetti sauce on her yellow vest," Lisa said. "And you know how spaghetti-sauce spots never come out."

"Yes, that was totally heartbreaking," Stevie said, pretending to wipe a tear from her eye. "Those long, dribbly red streaks."

"They went with her red fingernails," Lisa said.

"The ones that weren't broken," said Carole with a grin.

Veronica had brushed her gel-stiffened hair so vigorously that she had snapped a couple of nails.

The Saturday night celebration had, in fact, been pretty outstanding. Max had made a huge pot of spaghetti and his special sauce, Max's Mouthwatering Marinara. Deborah made garlic bread from a recipe she had gotten when she was working as a reporter in Italy. Mrs. Reg made her Salad Supreme, which was so good that even salad haters liked it.

There had been an award ceremony in which Max presented Jessica with a magnifying glass like the one that Sherlock Holmes used; Jackie with a deerstalker hat, like the one Sherlock wore; and Amie with a pipe, like the one Sherlock smoked. The only difference was that Amie's pipe was a bubble pipe. The younger kids had wound up running around chasing bubbles.

The older riders were in a great mood because the pretend mystery had been solved, which meant that they didn't owe the D.C. a day of work. In fact, everyone except Veronica was in an excellent mood.

Phil had worn his one-armed red sweater to the party, which made him a big hit with the younger children. He sat next to Stevie and said that he liked being a thief so much he was thinking about taking up a life of crime.

Stevie said that if he did that, The Saddle Club would have to take up detection on a permanent basis.

A.J. and Bart admitted that they had known all along that Phil was the "thief." They hadn't tried to solve the crime, but had just gone out on trail rides around Pine Hollow. Phil had brought Nickel to the rear paddock at night to sleep. When A.J. had come downstairs on Friday night—supposedly to admire the moonlight—he was trying to prevent The Saddle Club from going out to the paddock because he knew that Nickel was there.

"Imagine if we'd found Nickel," Lisa said. "The MW would have been over."

"I thought A.J. was completely loony, talking about the moonlight like that," said Carole.

"Phil told me he thinks A.J. *is* completely loony, but he likes him anyway," Lisa said. "Apparently A.J. reminds him a lot of Stevie!" The three girls laughed.

"You know what the best part of the whole weekend was?" said Stevie. "When Veronica found out that Phil had been sleeping in Max's guest bedroom."

"Her chin dropped," Carole said.

"Her lower lip went out," cried Lisa.

"She was going to call her father," Stevie said. "She said that Max was being unfair."

"Veronica nearly fainted when she found out that Phil had taken a hot shower," Carole said.

"And shampooed!" Stevie said. They all laughed, remembering Veronica's domed hair.

"She was so upset, she . . ." Lisa was laughing so hard she couldn't go on.

"Sat in the onion dip," Carole finished for her.

The girls were silent for a moment as they contemplated the magnificent memory of the expression on Veronica's face when she stood up and felt the onion dip ooze down her breeches into her boots.

"I'll always think of her that way," Lisa said.

Then Stevie remembered finding her saddle. "I'll never forget going into the barn and seeing all those saddles. It was creepy."

After the ambulance took the thief away, the police, Max, Phil, and The Saddle Club had gone to inspect the ramshackle barn where the thief had kept his horse. There had been at least a dozen saddles, including May Grover's and Stevie's. All of them were new or almost new. And there had been half a dozen bridles. Max had said that altogether the stolen tack was worth thousands of dollars. The thief must have been haunting the roads and trails in the woods for weeks.

"What a way to make a living," Stevie said.

"One more day and he and the saddles would have been gone forever," Carole said.

Max had told the girls that a used-tack auction was scheduled for the next day in a neighboring county. The police were sure that the thief meant to sell the stolen saddles there. Once the saddles were sold, there would have been almost no way to recover them.

"It just goes to show," Carole said. "Nameplates on a saddle are not enough."

The girls knew that at the next Horse Wise meeting Max was going to help them permanently identify their tack. One saddle thief had been caught, but there were more around.

"I learned something important," Lisa said.

"What's that?" asked Stevie.

"Our horses did all kinds of maneuvers. Like a standing jump," Lisa said. "I didn't know Prancer could do that."

"And backing up into bushes," said Carole. "I wasn't sure Starlight would do it."

"And Belle narrowly missed jumping into a tree," Stevie said. "I don't know what you call that maneuver, but I definitely appreciated it."

"It was the hardest riding I ever did," Carole said. "Because there were no rules. We had to figure everything out for ourselves."

"And convince Prancer, Starlight, and Belle that it was a good idea," Stevie added. "A couple of times I could tell that Belle thought I was crazy."

"But she went along with you because she trusts you," Carole said. "I guess it's what Max is always trying to teach us—a good rider can cope with the unexpected."

Lisa nodded. "When I realized that Prancer had to go all out, I was terrified. But then I trusted her, and she trusted me, and everything was fine. Although," she giggled, "I did have strange dreams last night. Race cars. Motorcycles."

"A speed demon is born," Stevie said.

Carole licked the last bit of vanilla ice cream off her spoon. "I've been thinking, too. You know the secret of The Saddle Club's success?"

"Brilliance?" said Stevie.

"Not exactly," said Carole with a grin.

"Bravery?" Lisa said.

"Not precisely," said Carole. "When you think about it, the main ingredient of our success on the MW was dumb luck."

"*What?*" said Stevie indignantly.

"It's true. If we hadn't mixed up the real and fake mysteries, we would never have caught the real thief," Carole said. "And if we hadn't thought the barred hoofprints were one of Max's brilliant clues, we would never have followed them."

"We could have missed out on all the glory," Lisa said.

"Actually, there isn't all that much glory," Stevie said.

"We're going to get our picture in *The Willow Creek Gazette*," Lisa finally said.

"On the back page," Carole said.

"My brother Chad told me The Saddle Club mishandled the whole thing. He said he could have caught the thief in half the time," Stevie said with a snort.

"You know what's truly great?" said Lisa.

"What's that?" Carole said.

"The group picture Deborah took of the MW gang," Lisa said.

"Yes," Carole said dreamily. "That's an excellent photograph."

"No," Stevie said, "it's *the* greatest photograph in the history of mankind."

At the end of the Mystery Weekend Deborah had taken the traditional photo of the participants, which was now hanging in the tack room next to those of previous MW groups. This one included the marvelous sight of Veronica diAngelo with broken fingernails, puffy, stiff hair filled with seeds, spaghetti-sauce stains on her vest, and—best of all—onion dip oozing into her boots.

"The miserable expression on Veronica's face will keep me going through the long winter ahead," Stevie said.

"It's something to live for," Carole said.

"It was one crazy weekend," Lisa said happily. "You know what the real mystery is? How we can ever top it!"

ABOUT THE AUTHOR

BONNIE BRYANT is the author of many books for young readers, including novelizations of movie hits such as *Teenage Mutant Ninja Turtles®* and *Honey, I Blew Up the Kid*, written under her married name, B. B. Hiller.

Ms. Bryant began writing The Saddle Club in 1986. Although she had done some riding before that, she intensified her studies then and found herself learning right along with her characters Stevie, Carole, and Lisa. She claims that they are all much better riders than she is.

Ms. Bryant was born and raised in New York City. She still lives there, in Greenwich Village, with her two sons.

Look for Bonnie Bryant's next exciting Saddle Club book . . .

WESTERN STAR
Super Edition #3

The girls of The Saddle Club can't wait for winter break from school. Carole, Stevie, and Lisa are heading west to spend the first part of their vacation at one of their favorite places—the Bar None Ranch.

But what they thought would be a quick trip turns into a snowbound adventure. The girls must rescue a herd of horses that are facing a terrible fate. . . .

Join The Saddle Club on an unforgettable trip that recalls the true spirit of giving and the strength of friendship.